Spontaneous Writing

by
TWENTY
COURAGEOUS WRITERS

Spontaneous Writing

by

**TWENTY
COURAGEOUS WRITERS**

published by
Wide Awake Publishing
Sequim, WA

Spontaneous Writing
by Twenty Courageous Writers

Copyright 2018

ALL RIGHTS RESERVED
PRINTED IN THE UNITED STATES OF AMERICA

Published by Wide Awake Publishing, Sequim, WA • wideawakepublishing.com

PARTICIPATING AUTHORS:

Gordon Anderson, Glen Barbieri, Cheryle Hoskins Bigelow,
Patricia DeMarco, Bonnie Dickmann, Susan Geis, Heidi Hansen,
Dianne L. Knox, Judy Larimore, Philip Libott, Anne Lizborne,
Ruth Marcus, Trudy McFarland, George Miller, Neva Miller, Terry Moore,
Vykki Morrison, Colin Sellwood, Lily Todd, Jim Weatherly

ISBN 978-0-9766004-6-6 Perfect Bound
Designed by Ruth Marcus
Type set in Minion

TABLE OF CONTENTS

PREFACE

Twenty courageous writers submitted writings for this anthology.
Over the course of two-and-a-half years, close to two-hundred prompts
have been used in our writing sessions. We hope you are inspired by
these creative, spontaneous writings.

——

WHAT IS SPONTANEOUS WRITING? An adventure—a playful, freestyle writing inspired by a prompt. The titles in the Table of Contents of this book are prompts used by the twenty writers published in this anthology.

I encourage you to experience the process. Open your writing journal. Set a timer for ten minutes. Choose a prompt and begin to write—spontaneously! Don't let self-judgement stop you. Don't worry about spelling and grammar. When the timer rings, take a deep breath and rest your pen.

What did you notice? Were you able to relax and let the words flow without judgement? Was it fun, challenging, inspiring?

Writers love to be inspired. Spontaneous writing helps us relax and take risks. No goals, no planning. Write for the joy and freedom of words and ideas flowing spontaneously. Surprise yourself—from wild and crazy, to passionate and poetic, stretch your boundaries. Create characters. Practice dialogue. Write stories and poems. Write nonsense.

Next step? Read your writing aloud. This process frees us from self-judgment. In a group of spontaneous writers, it teaches us to appreciate the diversity of what one prompt can produce. You learn writing tips and build confidence with other writers.

I want to extend a pat on the back to the twenty courageous writers who have contributed to this book. There is a prompt and the author's name on every page. This anthology demonstrates the range of creativity produced by simple prompts. Who knows? These writings may evolve over time.

When I organized the Spontaneous Writing Group in 2015, I listened to the needs and suggestions of writers:

- *I don't want to commit to showing up every month.*
- *Can it be free?*
- *No critiques, please.*
- *I don't want a discussion group.*
- *Needs to be friendly and supportive.*

Writers are similar and different in their needs. Simple guidelines work: No fee. No critiques. No need to RSVP—arrive on time. Oh yes, be willing to wear a name tag (first name only). And, be willing to write—even if its gobbledegook.

We read what we write. This rattles the nerves, but inspires courage. Confidence grows as we listen to our unique writing styles. And yes, we are free to pass if we choose.

A library or community center is a perfect setting for a free writing and reading venue—a quiet room with comfortable chairs arranged in a circle. Did you know that a circle promotes equality and inclusion? We write, we read, then leave—inspired and energized. Yes, we welcome guests.

Experience the joy of spontaneous writing! Join us, or create a group with your friends.

RUTH MARCUS
Facilitator of Spontaneous Writing

Note: We thank the Sequim Library for providing a room for this free writing venue that welcomes all levels of writers. We encourage you to support your local library.

*Spontaneous
Writing*

A BAG OF MONEY / WATER DAMAGE / SEA GULLS

by PATRICIA DEMARCO

SEAGULLS CIRCLED HIGH ABOVE the field for several days following unusual monsoon-type late fall rains that inundated the field. The rains were beginning to abate, allowing the waters to recede. The soil had been wet and cold for weeks causing the crops to suffer, turning anemic pale yellow and green. Plants grew stunted and many sprouts washed away. Screeching gulls filled the air until they finally found enough space where a few landed and headed out into the muddy waters to dig out corpses drowned by the water… gophers, mice, earthworms, etc.

The farmers knew their crews could not work the fields for quite awhile so with resigned faces, they drove out to see other farms, to collectively talk water-damage insurance coverage. Other sightseers drove along the country road wondering about the crops, as well.

Birders scouted for bird life drawn to the mayhem. One particular hummock drew not only gulls, but crows, a few stalwart ravens and a couple of bald eagles. A coyote had been sighted. Clearly they were eating something, perhaps a deer wounded by hunters, or a missing calf from the dairy across the road. A few days later, bones were clearly visible on the hummock's brow.

Someone called the sheriff's office and an officer was dispatched to investigate. Slowly he drove along the road, coming to a halt opposite the hummock. Already dressed in rain jacket and gum boots, he carefully made his way across the muddy flats, his steps slowed to give the avian life time to scatter. Reluctantly the birds lifted, settling in a few yards distant from the carcass.

The patrolman knelt down and picked up a stick that floated into the field from the hedgerow, using it to lift a nylon backpack, its zippers open to reveal it was a bag of money, all bills, all damp and lumpy. The officer glanced over at the bones, clearly a partially decomposed human male corpse. He stood, reached into his own pocket, pulled out a cell phone and called into his office.

A BAG OF MONEY / WATER DAMAGE / SEA GULLS

by GEORGE MILLER

THE TABLE WAS SPREAD before them all. He and his extended family were seated at the 12-foot-long dining table, heaped high with the Thanksgiving feast. Glistening table ware, sumptuous dishes, every glass filled, everyone smiling, and he, honored, seated at the head of the table. His heart and senses were filled. To his right, his father stood, raised his glass then spoke when the room quieted.

"Thank you all for joining us today to celebrate our blessing and supreme joy at the safe return of our son." He turned to his son, and smiling even more broadly, announced that he had a special gift for his son. From below the table, he lifted a wrapped package, handed it over, asking it to be opened right then. Surprised, the son peeled back the ribbon and paper, opened the box and saw bundles of $100 bills— more money than he'd ever seen in his life. The father explained that, since the son had opted to join the service, the college fund had been invested and it had done very, very well. Now the son was financially set to begin the next stage of his life, no matter what he chose to do.

The son was suddenly overcome. His eyes began to tear, overwhelmed by the overflowing love and blessings heaped up, piled high. Then, unexpectedly dizzy, several family members rushed to his side to ease his fall as he collapsed to the floor and then blacked out.

An instant later, he began to regain consciousness. He first sensed intense heat, then a gentle rocking, and then the voices of those around him, first soothing, then turning harsh, blaring, and sharp. He jolted awake by a sharp poke at his right eye and a sharp pain on his right arm. In anger and reflex, his right hand lifted to protect his eye and arm, and he jerked his head to the right. Opening his eyes, he could only sense a great whirling and intense glare. Then he heard a great roar punctuated by shrill screams. Panicked, disoriented, he shifted his whole body to the right, bumped something soft but unyielding. Repelled, revolted, he shifted quickly left as his eyes began to focus and adjust to the intense light and the surrounding commotion. The screaming seemed to diminish. Quickly looking left and right from his prone position, he saw a low barrier all around him, and below him a floor, but not a floor. Above him, in the intense light, more fluttering…a flurry of white and blue. What? What is this? Where am I?

Sensing momentary safety, and giving himself the relief of a deep, full breath, he attempted to calm as he looked all around himself again. Taking stock, he saw a small, fresh cut on his right bicep. He felt moisture (blood?) on his right eye. It hurt, and his vision was blurred. Looking up again, the flurry started to become familiar. Leaves, branches blowing in the wind? No, birds. Bird wings. White bird wings against a blue background. Seagull wings. A dozen seagulls flapping overhead, all focused on him, screeching, diving, then retreating just beyond arm's reach. The rocking….Water? The walls…the floor, solid yet not solid. Lifting his head slightly, he could see movement of dark blue shifting mountains beyond the walls.

In that instant, he relived the terror recalling his plane, crippled by gun fire, crashing to the water seven long days ago and how he'd been adrift in this raft since then. In the next instant, he was jolted by the bump of something large against his body through the flimsy cloth floor of his raft.

prompt
A DIALOGUE BETWEEN YOU AND A CAB DRIVER

by GEORGE MILLER

"HOW YOU doin' today? Heading uptown or down?"

"I'm not sure….I need to get to 2715 River Drive."

"You new to town?"

"Obvious, huh?"

He chuckled, and my instinct told me he smelled fresh meat and a big fare.

"Yeah. It's obvious….That's about a 15-minute ride with traffic today. So it'll just be a few bucks. Or, if you want to treat yourself, we can take the scenic route. There's a lot to see here in the city. It's a great place with lots to see and it is a beautiful day."

I was tired from my long cross-country flight. The fatigue increased by my thinking about my new assignment here, all I'd left behind for the duration, and anxiety from the crushing workload I was about to take on.

Somehow, my mind drifted and I was back on my first roller-coaster ride and the anxiety of that slow ascent as the coaster ratcheted seemingly inch by inch upward, to that point at the apex, where all I saw was sky, and beyond only the unknown, no doubt to certain death. With each second, my fear mounted—nine years old, ready to cry, trapped in the very front seat with my 12-year-old cousin, Rusty. How did I get myself into this?

"Rusty, I'm scared! I want to get off!!"

"Yeah! Isn't it great? But forget about it—just put that out of your head—there's no stopping now!"

"What? NO!!! I want to get off!" I screamed as we reached the top, and all I could see was sky ahead.

Over the all mounting screams of the giggles behind us he shouted, "You're not in danger, you're just scared. Stand up to it. You'll see it's nothing. Fly through it. Fly. See how brave you can be. Give me your hand!"

Thinking he was giving me some way to calm me and protect me, I placed my hands in his, and to my terror, he lifted our hands over our heads as we fell over the top.

I never screamed so loud—or laughed—so hard. A mere two-minute lifetime later, as the car slowed to a stop, I shouted, "Let's ride again!" And we did—20 times that day.

I recalled that, even with that excitement and thrill, every ride to some sort of "top" throughout my life had brought back that brief jolt of terror, and they had always been followed by consummate exhilaration, both at the ride, and the pride that I'd held and called the bluff, faced down the ghost and walked through those illusory walls of fire to the gift of what was beyond.

That holding had served me well in life since and brought me so much of life that I knew I would have missed otherwise. There had been many other bluffs and mirages since and they'd all become obvious to me when, in standing to confront them, a guide had presented itself to me to show me the way through and beyond.

I came back to the cab, and the driver facing me from the front seat, waiting for his answer.

"You know, I'll bet you've got some great stories about this place. I'm going to be here a while, and this will be a great way to learn about my new home. You've got a deal on the scenic route. Thanks for the offer. Drive on."

prompt

A DOOR LEFT OPEN

by PATRICIA DeMARCO

CLUCKY CHICKEN APPROACHED the normally shut chicken coop door, peering through a crack created when a gust of squirrelly springtime wind blew through. She felt the urge to push her beak into the crack widening it even more, encouraged to take advantage of a door left open and the new digs she saw beyond looking full of discovery and eating potential.

The plucky, red hen stuck her beak into the crack and pushed. The door creaked on its dusty hinges but opened enough to reveal even more of the cornucopia of feasting awaiting her. She repositioned herself and properly put her bulky body sideways and pushed. The lightweight door gave way, swinging open at the precise moment a grasshopper hopped into view. Clucky Chicken was off and running. Another squirrelly gust slammed the door shut, knocking the closure lever securely in place. Not that she ever looked back.

In no time she'd found the garden, fenced for deer and cows but not chickens. Her feet flew into action in the soft soil, unlike the hard-packed outdoor pen where she spent her days. Very soon she had created a trail of mayhem. No longer in rows, the lettuce, basil, and scraggly carrots lie strewn about the cauliflower and broccoli plants, all tipped on their sides. It appeared as if a tornado had touched down in the strawberries. Shredded leaves and partially-eaten berries littered the ground.

Satiated, the plump hen scooped a depression in the raspberry rows and immersed herself in the soft duff. What her day of freedom will cost her is for the fates to decide but scraping the dry soil and wood fibers over her body, she thought of nothing else but after a short break to start where she left off.

by HEIDI HANSEN

IT WAS BECAUSE of the door left open that the cat ran out of the house. At first, content with its escape, it sat on the lawn preening. Then it chased a bird up the tree in a neighboring yard.

Because the cat climbed the tree, it sat mewing on the branch after the bird got away. The cat appeared to be waiting to be rescued. Because the cat sat in the tree, crows cawed, screeching at the intruder. This noise alerted two black labs sniffing about the street. They detected the cat in the tree and started barking.

Eloise Davis resided in the house near the tree now inhabited by the cat. She heard the barking dogs. Being afraid of dogs, she called a neighbor for help.

"Whose dogs?" Bill Brown, the neighbor asked.

"Why are they barking at my tree?" Eloise asked.

Bill Brown tried to help. He approached the dogs with pepper spray but found the dogs friendly. When they stopped barking, he heard the cat.

"Whose cat?" he asked.

By now Alice Stuart and her sister Mary had come outside from across the street and looked into the tree at the cat. Because the cat was usually kept indoors, no one recognized it.

"Get a ladder," Alice said.

"Call the fire department," Mary said.

As the onlookers grew in number, the owner of the cat, Marge Black, looked out her window. "What's going on?" she said. When she found her front door open, she realized her cat had escaped.

"Help," she called from the doorway.

Several of the neighbors hurried over to her.

"What's wrong?" Bill Brown asked.

"Call 911," Mary said.

"My cat is missing," Marge said.

At that moment, a fire truck pulled onto the street, sirens blaring. Two police cruisers followed. Then came the local television station news van. Firemen jumped from the truck and unwound hoses. The captain addressed the crowd, "Where's the fire?"

"No fire," said Bill Brown.

"No fire?" repeated the fireman.

"It's a cat," Alice Stuart said pointing up the tree.

"A cat?" the firemen said in unison.

"The cat is stuck in the tree."

As every eye peered at the tree, the black and white cat clambered down, jumped onto the walkway and confidently walked home, entering through the door left open.

A DOOR LEFT OPEN

by N E V A   M I L L E R

SHOULD I STEP THROUGH, I knew there would be no turning back.

They say if you leap off a cliff, you will sprout wings and fly away. I had truly believed that, I thought, until I was faced with my dilemma.

The wall was dark and imposing, sizzling hot to the touch in the 110 degrees with no shade to be found. The door was rusty, caked with dust and forced open, somehow, just wide enough for a body to squeak through without losing too much skin in the process.

My small, faded backpack held the contents of everything left of my life…a few items of clothing and an old photo of my once-family.

Considering my life, like watching an old black and white film, I tossed the backpack through the gap, kicked aside the crackling, dry tumbleweed used to disguise the door, and squeezed through the opening into the unknown.

I stepped gingerly into the foreign place. Hoping and praying that my limited Spanish would be enough to start my new life South of the Border.

AIRPLANE / PAPERCLIPS

by CHERYLE HOSKINS BIGELOW

I HOPE THE AIRPLANE I board doesn't suck a goose into an engine like my new vacuum cleaner sucked up the paperclips scattered on the rug near my writing desk.

Yes, it would be scary to fall out of the sky, even though I always try to sit in an aisle seat in a row with an emergency exit in the rear of the plane, and I avoid wearing polyester in case of fire.

But replacing a vacuum cleaner was my bad. It couldn't be blamed on a flock of geese.

AIRPLANE / PAPERCLIPS

by RUTH MARCUS

HENRY, WITH STRAW-COLORED HAIR, and Maurice, with black curly hair, tip-toed away from the fourth grade class trip that was touring the XYZ Toy Company in Dubuque, Iowa. Rounding the corner, they ducked into the men's room, both giggling with hands over their mouths.

"Shut up, Maury. We'll get caught," Henry said as he unzipped his pants and peed.

"Hurry up," said Maury as Henry waved his hands in front of the faucet, then squirted Maury. He quacked like a duck, then waved his hands to activate the hand dryer. The boys peaked out the door to make sure no one was in the hallway.

"Come on Maury. I'm taking you to my dad's office so you can see the airplanes he designs."

"Airplanes? Airplanes?" Maury was known to repeat things twice.

"Yes, my dad designs airplanes in his free time."

"You're joking," Maury said poking Henry in his arm.

The boys tip-toed like criminals sneaking up on a victim—shoulders pulled up around their ears, exaggerating each step.

"I'm not kidding you. My father makes a fortune designing toys for kids. He brought home a prototype last week and told me it's going to be the hottest toy this year—paper clip airplanes.

"Ya-a-a, right," Maury said. "Do you believe everything your father says?"

"Why shouldn't I?" Henry rolled his eyes, his forehead furrowed like a skillfully carved pumpkin. "Follow me."

A brass plate stamped John Schmitt, CEO, was mounted on the polished hardwood door. Henry pulled it open, leaned in, then signaled, "Come on, Maury."

Sunlight streamed through a floor to ceiling window spotlighting the corner of the massive desk that looked out over downtown Dubuque. There it was, on the desk, a shiny airplane sculptured of paper clips. "Wow!" Maury said, reaching to touch it. As he pulled one clip, the entire plane leaned. "It's held together by a magnet," Henry said, pointing to the square box below the plane. Maury pulled with a little more force and the paper clips dipped and bowed.

"Oh no! Now look what you've done, Maury. We're in deep doo-doo."

"I can fix it. I can fix it." Maury said, using both hands in an attempt to return the paper clips to the shape of an airplane.

"Come on, we have to get out of here," Henry said. "If we get found out, I'll be grounded or something worse."

Maury laughed as they raced down the hall, avoiding the voice calling, "Henry...Maurice..."

The boys ducked into a stairwell. "I thought your dad was a hot shot toy designer. All he does is play with paper clips."

A MEMORABLE FIRST TRIP

by ANNE LIZBORNE

I LEFT MENDOCINO, CA for Baja, Mexico on the first solo trip I ever took to a foreign country. Mexico didn't seem very far away until I headed South on CA HWY 1. It quickly became clear my bright blue, Metro Chevy had a long haul ahead of her, final destination Cabo San Lucas, Baja, Mexico. I named my car "Ocean." It was just right for the 3,000 mile trip along the Pacific. Anything could happen, and did. I was ready for adventure. Mystery was part of the draw.

Little "Ocean" got 70 mpg on gas, astronomical at the time, so I knew I could count on an inexpensive trip. What I hadn't known was that gas stations were sparse south of the Rio Grande. I topped off the tank every chance I got and carried a 10 gallon can of gas tied to the back of the car, just in case. As it turned out I would need the gas in trade for auto repair services. Like a fool, I locked my keys in the car at a beachfront campground thinking desperate Mexicans would surely attempt to rob me if I left the car open. I was wrong. They not only didn't rob me, they saved me from my own insane fear by showing how easy it was to break into a car, handing me the keys with a smile. I thanked them with the can of gas. We parted as friends. That was just one of the good things that happened along the way. Mexican hospitality opened my heart to many more kind encounters.

The drive down Baja was long, dry, hot, and totally unpredictable. One stretch was well kempt and not much different from driving in southern California, USA. Mid-point along the Peninsula was another story, that's when the road and terrain got rough. By then, I was one of a few people on the road and the only solo, female driver. It was getting dark and there were no hotels, campgrounds, towns, or gas stations in sight. My fear barometer was running red hot. What to do?

One of the things I learned along the way was that sign language, a good translation dictionary, and local maps could get me through the basics. Need food, point to mouth and rub stomach. Need a toilet, jump up and down, point to your privates, and look desperate. Need a taxi, flag one down, open your map, point to where you want to go, and trust them to take you there. Trust is the hard part, but it works.

When a group of Mexican men showed up at my window while I was parked on the side of a dark road looking totally lost, which I was, my life passed before my eyes. I knew it would soon be over. Then they took out their flashlight along with their Spanish to English dictionary and asked if I needed help. "YES," I said while breathing a sign of relief!! They then pointed me in the right direction and filled my tank with gas enough from their truck to get me to the next town. It's untrue that most people can't be trusted. From then on I always gave strangers the benefit of the doubt until proven otherwise and they did the same back to me. I like most people and they know it.

Traveling solo through the world taught me to trust people and my intuition. When I do that, I rarely go wrong. I'm so glad for that first solo trip to Baja. By facing fear of solo travel, my heart and mind opened to the world. All I needed to travel safely was basic good sense and a willingness to listen to my intuition and heart. Other women I met along the way asked if I were not afraid to travel alone? I always said of course I sometimes am, but that doesn't keep me from doing it. If you long to travel you'll do it no matter what. If something goes wrong, that's ok too. Fear will never again run my life nor keep me locked behind metal bars on the windows and heavy duty deadbolts on the door.

My world travels have taken me everywhere imaginable. I've solo traveled by boat, car, bush plane, RV, rickshaw, train, and chicken buses overloaded with people and things going to market. I've prayed to live for just one more trip through a few dangerous countries, but everywhere I've gone my feeling about people remained the same. Some people are truly dangerous and best avoided, while others are angels that would give you the shirts off their backs. Most people are somewhere in the middle, myself included, and can be counted on for help. As long as I have my hands to sign with, a good translation book to aid with communication, and a reliable compass and map, all will be well. I've never regretted that first solo trip to Mexico. It opened up the world.

prompt
AM I UNDER ARREST OR NOT?

by PATRICIA DEMARCO

"AM I UNDER ARREST or not?" the woman shouted, defiantly holding the protest sign in front of her. The line of armed guardsmen pulled back. Again she shouted, "Am I under arrest or not?" Eagle feathers adorned with beads braided into her long, black hair vibrated with an energy that conveyed: "I defy your orders to move us out!" The golden elk ivories sewn to the smoke-tanned elk leather vest chattered with every movement her strong body made. The guardsmen eyed each other, aware of their own gear, aware of helmets, infrared and body cameras, flack vests, armed rifles, Taser rods, canisters of this and that.

She could smell them, their fear, their hatred. "Go ahead and arrest me! I am unarmed!" She dropped her sign. The ornately carved, silver bracelets with turquoise and red coral inlays adorned her crossed wrists, an action beckoning the guardsmen to come forward, to respond.

One young guardswoman, dropped her own weapon, crossed the line formed by other guardsmen, their weapons and protective coverings, and picked up the woman's sign in support of the protest. Her voice shaking, she held it in front of her own body as a shield and shouted, "I am unarmed! Am I under arrest? Am I under arrest or not?"

AM I UNDER ARREST OR NOT?

by **JIM WEATHERLY**

SHE KNEW it was not normal, but it felt so good that she simply did not care what others thought about her. Jellybean had found herself this year and was not putting up with anyone's nonsense—even that from her husband. Standing barefoot with a barren fridge staring back at her, she let the soft light and chilly breeze wake her senses. They were out of food and she needed to go shopping, an act she had grown to despise over the years. Off with her robe, on with her sweatpants tucked into her favorite scuffed black boots idling by the back door. Blue sweatshirt stretched over hair wild as a wheat field and out the door with no bra underneath, she headed down to the town Thrifty.

"Jellybean, what on earth are you wearin'?" her friend Gladys whispered across the rotisserie counter.

"Whaa?!"

Gladys intentionally scanned her eyes foot to head, while carelessly stuffing two chicken legs in a sweaty plastic bag for another customer (also gawking at her best friend).

"These rags make me feel good. Am I under arrest, or not, mizzz fashion police?! Now stop judging my breasts and thighs and gimme that chicken!!!"

AN EMBARRASSING MOMENT

by HEIDI HANSEN

IT WAS THE END OF TERM, one oral report to be given to the class at least ten minutes in length. I had dreaded this from the beginning of the semester. Yet, here I was. The day had finally arrived. I had done the research, written the report and it had been favorably commented on by the instructor.

I had carefully written the speech, practiced it aloud night after night for the past week. I had carefully selected my outfit—something that helped me seem credible on the topic. I dressed slowly that morning taking my time with my hair and makeup. I reviewed the speech once more and tucked the notes into my pocket. I felt ready—not as terrified as I had been, certainly not overly confident, but braced.

Class was at 1:30 and Tommy said, "Let's go to Taco Bell for lunch." He knew I liked the food there and it was close by.

As I took my seat, the instructor called out the order for the speeches. When it was my turn, I took the podium, made eye contact with the members of the audience. I straightened my notes and felt a familiar rumble in my intestines. Lord, not now, I prayed. I cleared my throat and was about to begin my report, when I farted.

AN EMBARRASSING MOMENT

by JUDY LARIMORE

THE TALLEST BUILDING in the world, the Burj Khalifa in Dubai, on January 11, 2016, was the setting for an embarrassing moment. A friend, Mary, and I decided to use the restroom before going up in the elevator to the 125th floor for spectacular views.

The symbol outside the restroom door looked like it had on a skirt indicating it was a women's restoom. When I came out of the stall there were six men waiting inside near the doorway. I looked at them with surprise on my face when I immediately realized the mistake we had made interpreting the symbol by the door. Without missing a beat I said, "Smile, I want to remember this." They all smiled as I quickly washed my hands, reached in my purse, pulled out my camera and captured the moment.

I walked past them through the doorway and waited for Mary to come out. She didn't. She stayed in the stall as I called out, "Mary we went in the men's restroom." It seemed like an eternity before she appeared. I said, "Why did you stay in there so long?" She said I couldn't move." I imagine those guys had fun telling their wives what happened to us.

The next embarrassing moment happened an hour later. After a rapid ride in the elevator with blue lights flashing, we were at the top of the gleaming, silver, Burj Khalifa looking at 360-degree views of Dubai. We could see our Royal Caribbean cruise ship in the distance.

The line to get back on the elevator was a very long wait. A uniformed woman told us that if we walked down a flight of stairs there was another elevator with no line. Several of us went down the stairs to the waiting empty elevator. I noticed when the lady opened the door and we all went in, packed like sardines, it was a plain box and no flashing lights. At five foot tall and at the back, everyone was taller than me. I did ask after we hadn't moved for several minutes if there was a button to push. No answer.

After ten more minutes went by to ease the tension I asked how many different languages we had among the group. It was five. Another few minutes went by and the tension was noticeable. I said, "Let's bang on the door behind us." We did, nothing happened. We did it again, louder. This time the door opened and the same lady that had put us in the elevator was still there. We hadn't moved. She said, "Did anyone at the front push G for ground?" We all stared laughing and were embarrassed but glad we were on our way this time.

A STRANGER TAPS YOU ON THE SHOULDER

by HEIDI HANSEN

A STRANGER TAPPED ME on the shoulder. I turned in my seat to see a middle-aged man in a three-piece suit.

"Is that your bag?" he asked.

I looked down to see a dark green grocery bag that lay partially under my seat.

"No," I said.

"It's moving," he said.

We both looked at the bag. It was a canvas tote, like the ones we use now to carry our groceries home. It was indeed wiggling.

Mid-afternoon, the subway car was not crowded. The seat beside me was unoccupied as were the two in front of me. The man sat behind me alone. I looked around. There seemed to be no one watching. I pulled the bag out from under the seat and opened it. Of course, I wanted to know what was inside the bag, but also, if there was any identification of the owner.

As I opened the tote bag, I clearly saw what was inside. A newborn baby wrapped tightly in a bright pink blanket.

The baby, a girl I presumed, stretched her arms, kicked her legs all contained within that swaddled blanket, but she was waking up. She was about to make her presence heard.

The man and I exchanged looks of surprise and looked again at the other passengers. No one seemed interested or watching what we would do. The car came to a stop and the man and I both rose. Was it our stop or were we fleeing the responsibility for the baby? At the last second I picked up the tote bag swinging the handles over my arm and stepped out onto the platform.

A STRANGER TAPS YOU ON THE SHOULDER

by GEORGE MILLER

IT WASN'T A STRANGER tapping my shoulder, but a book that called to me. After my mile-long hike through a blizzard to attend my night class, crossing fields and fording a small creek along the way.

The first to arrive, I settled into my desk after I shook the snow from my coat and book bag. After a moment, I saw a small paperback atop a desk on the opposite side of the room. I would have sworn it wasn't there when I scanned the room a moment before. After a few minutes more, with no one else yet arriving, I stepped across the room to give it a look.

Interesting cover and title. No evident sign of ownership. The pages plump with bent corners—the compliments and attention of many readings. Yet, desirable and prized, here it was, alone. Here we were, together, alone. I decided to sit and pass the time exploring a few of those selected pages until class started.

Forty pages later, I was pulled from the story by a tap at the room door. The janitor told me he needed to clean the room. He told me classes had been canceled due to the increasing storm, and I should head home. It seemed I was the only one who didn't get the message.

My attention returned from the story back to the room and then to my cold walk home. Reluctantly, I set the book down and got up from the chair and stepped across the room to get my book bag. Taking a step to the door, I looked back across the room. I'd never seen that book before—if I left it, would I see it again? Was it just coincidence that I found it? Would the owner, or some interloper claim it. After all, it was just sitting there waiting to be read. I stepped back, put the book in my bag, and headed out, now without concern for my long, cold walk back through the storm, anxious to be home, reading.

prompt
A SOUND (WRITE A SCENE BASED ON THE SOUND)

by PHILIP LIBOTT

HELICOPTER ROTOR BLADES

Over the house, so low that the whole frame structure vibrated, from roof to floor, and things shook loose from their moorings. Some empty jars slid off the living room table and onto the (fortunately) carpeted floor. The rotorcraft buzzed back and forth, back and forth, like some obsessed raptor over our heads. We weren't sure what they were looking for, what was it they were trying to find? Some illicit, illegal field mouse whose time was up?

A SOUND (WRITE A SCENE BASED ON THE SOUND)

by LILY TODD

A HEART WRENCHING SCREAM. Another one. A woman burst through the doors of the beauty salon like she was on fire.

The black cape fluttered behind her as she ran screaming through the Safeway parking lot. She gained momentum as she crossed row after row of parked cars. People everywhere stopped and stared at the fat lady shrieking so loudly. In awe we watched her bounce off a black 4x4 into a light blue Prius. Finally she stopped by a copper van.

The hair designer who followed her from the shop said "I didn't think the cut was that bad!"

by ANNE LIZBORNE

IT WAS 2AM on a moonlit night quiet as still water. Off in the distance an ambulance turned on its siren, piercing the air with the sound of Emergency. As the screaming ambulance came closer to home, the air suddenly split open with the sing-song sound of our local coyotes, followed by a back-up chorus of howling neighborhood dogs. This always happened when the ambulance turned on its siren. There's something about the shrieking sound that tells the coyotes to sing.

I live in the countryside, so the sudden appearance of coyotes is a special nighttime-only event. They awaken the coyote that lives inside me. I am soon wandering the meadow outside my back door to get closer to these wild critters, to sing-song with them under the blazing full moon. My neighbors think I'm crazy but I have yet to be threatened by these cunning, shadowy friends. The largest coyote often appears and disappears in the woodlands that skirt the meadow, giving the local cats a deserved scare. Their favorite meal seems to be rabbits or moles, not humans. I have great respect for wild animals and they know it. I don't invade their space, they don't invade mine, so we get along fine.

The sound of howling coyotes gets me howling too. Their crystalline songs turn an ordinary night into pure magic. I much prefer hearing singing coyotes to barking dogs in the middle of the night. Domestic dogs lack deep purpose, a meager substitute for the real thing. Coyotes hold nothing back as they full out answer the screaming ambulance, imagining they are the real Emergency, not some sorry human. They are no doubt right. Their music allows me to free the wild coyote inside. Tonight is a perfect time for Coyote Concert under a lush Full Moon. Sing on, my friends, sing on. It's time to get out my dancing feathers and drum. Won't you join me on the meadow? It's all right. Don't be afraid. We are, after all, One.

BOOKWORM / OVERLY LARGE GIFT

by GLEN BARBIERI

SKARN WAS DIGESTING another book. It was about frogs. That was the subject du jour. It was noisy in the orphanage, so it was hard to concentrate. She squinted her large, blue eyes.

"Get to tadpoles yet?" begged Bareli. The calico werecat looked expectantly at Skarn. "I like tadpoles. I like them wriggling between my toes."

The bookworm sighed. So much for privacy. Then again, Bareli was barely more than a kitten. That, plus her exuberance, was an overly large gift. What did she eat? Batteries?

"No, Bareli, haven't gotten to tadpoles. I'm reading about habitat."

Bareli blinked. "Habi-what-what?"

"Habitat. That's where they live."

"Oh. Like the Two moons? If I go to a moon, I want a pet frog."

Skarn pursed her lips. Where did that come from?

prompt
BOOKWORM / OVERLY LARGE GIFT

by DIANNE L. KNOX

VOLUMES

She spoke volumes
In appearance and speech
She was flamboyant in dress
Eyes made up like a dark actress
But, she was a book worm
Not bookish or wormish
Contradiction not wasted
Reading coming out in her looks
Meaning coming from
An overly large gift of books
This present her presence.

BOOKWORM / OVERLY LARGE GIFT

by PHILIP LIBOTT

BECAUSE SHE KNEW about my proclivity to occasionally create a minimalized life-space for myself as a bookworm, holed up inside the spare bedroom as a kind of low-rent and solitary atelier, she had ordered sixteen books about Early Colonial U.S. History for me via Amazon.com. It seemed to me, at the time, that it was an overly large gift. Looking at the box, I felt a reluctance to move towards the required dedication and commitment it would take to soldier through these volumes. I knew I'd easily morph into a focused student of history and triangulator of how distant 18th Century European conflicts translated into rural, frontier skirmishes on the multiple edges of these "new world" empires, but understood that this cerebral adventure would be an arduous, and yet altogether noble undertaking. I tore apart the four glued, cardboard flaps on the top of the box, picked up the first book on the stack, and started reading.

by A N N E   L I Z B O R N E

ACCORDING TO FAMILY HISTORY, my life as a bookworm began with reading the *Encyclopedia Britannica for Children* while sitting on the commode waiting to poop. That was Mother's toilet training strategy for two-year-olds. Her strategy worked. I later became the first College grad in our family, a lifetime reader, a wannabee writer, and a good pooper in the right places at the right times.

The encyclopedia was filled with strange words and exotic pictures, igniting my 2-year-old imagination. I can't think of a better way to begin life. It introduced me to everything on and off Planet Earth. I especially loved pictures and stories about animals. My favorite animals were horses.

I was born to be a horsewoman. I collected horse pictures and toys, dreamed about riding them, and longed to have one. My standard outfit was Wrangler blue jeans, leather chaps, a bright, orange cowboy hat, shiny black cowboy boots, and a six shooter cap gun strapped to my pre-adolescent waist. Roy Rodgers, Gene Autry, The Lone Ranger, and Zorro were my Heroes. Everyone in town thought I was a very odd girl but I didn't care. The only thing I cared about besides my dog Cheena, my brassy gold trumpet, and my High Flyer Blue Boys Bike, was getting a horse all my own.

Mary Hoose, a rodeo riding friend from 4-H, told me how to get a horse for free. One day after 4-H she took me to her neighbors ranch where I was told one of their horses was looking for a new home. The horse's name was "Charley." Charley was a gentle, retired, 20-year-old Palamino Quarter Horse who had once been a Champion Rodeo Barrel Racer and Round-up Pony. I took one look into Charley's large, old, soft, friendly brown eyes and said, "Yes, I'll take him!!"

I was nine years old, had never ridden a horse, but knew all about them thanks to the *Encyclopedia Britannica for Children*. The only obstacle to claiming Charley was convincing my parents I just HAD to have him!! Were they ever surprised when Mary's funky, green pick-up truck and Horse Trailer arrived at our front door the next day. Charley was inside!! Mary just KNEW I had to have that horse!! So Charley came home, and home Charley stayed, and that's when life really began to make sense!!

Many horses came and went out of my life after good, old, faithful Charley, but Charley was my favorite, my first real dream come true, the best and biggest gift of my life. Thank you *Encyclopedia Britannica for Children*, Mary Hoose, and Mom and Dad for listening to my aching 9-year-old heart and saying, "YES!!"

BOOKWORM / OVERLY LARGE GIFT

by JIM WEATHERLY

THE BOOKWORM INCHED and stretched his way out between pages 105 and 106 to greet the morning. Rob had learned over the years to hunker and sleep in the margins—less ink to wash off later in the library's water fountain. Every other fluorescent light flickered and hummed above. As he homed in on the backroom sorting shelves across the children's wing, Rob faintly smelled cinnamon. A signal that only Sarah had arrived so far for the day.

Today, though, he caught the scent of something else. Something new. There, on the checkout counter, sat an overly large, bright orange globe. He reached for his specs. Rob now saw more clearly the pumpkin.

"Ah...," he thought to himself, "what a gift this time of year can be."

BOOKWORM / OVERLY LARGE GIFT

by TERRY MOORE

EVER THE BOOKWORM, and on the lookout for gems of the written word, I was on the road in Washington State during the season of flowers, and went to the small coastal town of La Conner for lunch. Afterwards, needing to walk off my lunch, I took a turn down an interesting looking alley. Two buildings down, across from Alice's antiques, I found myself staring straight into the eyes of George Washington. His eyes were clear and blue, attention getting, and each was about a foot high.

Someone had carved a cedar likeness of George Washington's head that measured about nine feet high. A stroke of brilliance inspired me to find the owner. "It's free," he said. "Just haul it away." A friend owned a low forty-foot tractor trailer rig for hauling earthmoving equipment, and he owed me a favor. My brother-in-law in Kingston was in for a midnight surprise, an overly large gift accompanied by a book, a biography about the father of our country. I underlined two words in the intro to the book. Top this!

by PATRICIA DEMARCO

KEFIR, A FERMENTED CULTURE grown in raw milk, can be somewhat difficult to grow but once established, it multiplies at exponential rates eventually taking over the kitchen countertop with nuggets of creamy, raw milk flavor. I was at the point of having an abundance of kefir grains so the idea of using them in a gluten-free coffee cake for a harvest potluck we had been invited to seemed the smart thing to do. I've used kefir before usually in making a smoothie or draining it through cheesecloth for kefir cheese.

I love to fabricate and tweak recipes and usually have good success. In fact, for me to follow the same recipe twice exactly the same way is like stepping into the same river twice, it just can't be done. Perusing the internet, I discovered the perfect recipe and followed it in my own logical way, substituting spices, flavorings and honey for sugar compensating for moisture. So I was expecting there could be some discrepancies on baking time but found myself bordering on getting mad, downright outrageously mad as I noticed the cake was still gooey after the recipe's designated time was up. It had this creepy consistency, almost like drool. I put it back in the oven and turned up the heat. More time, another twenty minutes, and again.

Eventually time was totally up, I couldn't help it, we had to go. I tasted a spoonful. It had a rich ambrosial taste of spicy ginger and syrupy honey with mace. Finally I decided at least I'd make out a notecard listing the ingredients for people with allergies and call it good. Placing the cake in a tote tray, I wrapped it with my colorful potluck cloth and we were off.

Once there, I set it at the back of the dessert table thinking that the late arrivals or dessert addicts would at least have something. To my chagrin, probably a dozen people came to me asking about the ingredients and how I had come up with such a wonderful pudding-cake. I was speechless, but after recovering from my amazement, I told each inquirer the basics but gave no assurances it would come out the same. When I went to pickup the dish, it had been moved to the front and literally scraped clean. What an enormous boost to my culinary ego!

by DIANNE L. KNOX

SHOPPING

She zooms past my house
On her bike
Every day, yes, every
At 10:55 AM
Her return one hour later
Full sack hanging on her handlebar
Lunch? Or, simply exercise?

by PHILIP LIBOTT

FOUR-YEAR-OLD ASLYN very carefully carries, individually, each of the five pieces of the pink plastic, Disney Beauty and the Beast tea set (the teapot and the four cups) over to the large Brita water reservoir sitting by the kitchen sink, and then carefully, one by one, fills the teapot and cups with water from the spigot. Aslyn then very carefully, so as not to spill any water, separately carries each component back to the toy kitchen in the living room, and then prepares to serve tea to her guests.

DIVING DEEP

by SUSAN GEIS

THE ANTICIPATION of my first time diving was keeping me up nights before the event. My mind kept thinking about the fun, excitement, and dangers that could happen with this sport. I found myself restless and didn't sleep at all the night before. I had been invited along with about ten others but this was my first time diving. I was a little younger than the others so they had prior knowledge and experience. I had watched other people do this before but now it was finally my turn and I was afraid that I would make a complete fool of myself. I didn't want to appear clumsy or lacking in skill in front of the others—especially the guys. I also had another fear—my hair. I had long beautiful wavy hair that reached my waist, but when it got soaking wet it would frizz up worse than a Brillo Pad. Everyone showed up right on time at 6:30 sharp. There were seven guys and seven girls. To my surprise one guy actually flirted with me. He told me that he thought I looked hot in my 'mermaid' outfit.

The diving started and a few guys dove right in, head first, without fear. When it was my turn I held my hair back with one hand, took a deep breath and dove nose first into the water. I opened my mouth wide but foolishly got nothing but water! I remember the sun setting and the orange lanterns were lit with candles. It gave my dive an eerie dream-like quality. The next try was much better and I was able to latch onto one of the smaller red apples. Everyone was clapping when I came up with the red shiny apple in my mouth. The danger was over! I got an apple and my long beautiful hair stayed dry.

I also noticed the guy that said I looked hot in my mermaid outfit was dressed as a swashbuckling pirate. He eyes were on me as he walked towards me, weaving between the other people dressed up for the Halloween Costume Party.

I had survived bobbing for apples, but I wasn't' sure if I would survive the devastating brilliant smile from the handsome pirate.

**FAMILIAR ADDRESS:
WRITE A SCENE ASSOCIATED WITH THE ADDRESS**

by DIANNE L. KNOX

25 CLAYMORE ROAD

Twenty-two floors up, maids quarters
Marble floors, Singapore
Looking down at Orchard Road,
Jason's Grocery, Thai Embassy, Dynasty Hotel,
CK Tangs Department Store
Sounds, smells, a beautiful life
Watching nightly Tai Chi dancing
Flowing on Jason's rooftop
My breath coordinated with their play
Peregrine Falcons fly to the Thai Embassy
Their flight timed precisely
A pair mated for life
Coupling like me.

FAMILIAR ADDRESS:
WRITE A SCENE ASSOCIATED WITH THE ADDRESS

by JUDY LARIMORE

912 MAPLE BLVD., LIBERAL, KANSAS: October 1, 1967 was the day our family moved into our first real home. After seven rentals and lots of moves in our first years of marriage, during and after college, I was thankful for my parents help with the down payment. It was a 2,500 square foot, 20-year-old, stucco, cream-colored house with a wood shake roof. Across the street was a park, perfect for the kids. You had to look for a tree when you left town. That's why I loved the sixteen trees that surrounded our new home for the next eighteen years.

The day we moved in could be described as pretty hectic but I didn't notice, I was home at last. Our baby son, Dave, was eight weeks old on moving day. It was his sister, Kris' fourth birthday and his older sister, Kise was six.

In addition to boxes and furniture being moved into the house, my husband and I were setting up a swing set in the backyard for a birthday present for Kris. Dave was sleeping in his rocker seat because we hadn't had time to set up the crib.

At one end of the kitchen there was a built-in brown, oblong booth that would be our dinning area. It was surrounded by unpacked boxes. On the kitchen cabinet was a birthday cake with four candles waiting for the Happy Birthday song.

After the swing set was put together we all gathered at the booth around the unpacked boxes. Kise, our tomboy, was sitting next to

Kris, who in those days would be described as a girly girl. I have a photo of Kise with a play cowboy gun and holster and Kris with fluffy skirt and long bead necklaces. That describes them through the growing up years. Kise was teasing Kris and asking when we were going to sing Happy Birthday. I lit the candles and carried the cake to the table, hoping the baby wouldn't wake up before we sang Happy Birthday. Dave stayed asleep but just as we finished singing, the phone rang.

I hurriedly got up to answer before the ring woke the baby, moving boxes out of the way to make a path to the phone. "Hello." It was the president of an organization I was the vice president of asking me to do something. Amid the unpacked boxes, birthday celebration, and eight week old baby that had just gone to sleep I was able for the first time to say, "No I can't do that."

During those days of young motherhood, I sought approval because I didn't have the self-confidence I needed. The phone call should have been a turning point to realize I always said "Yes," no matter what. I would like to say I learned my lesson and could say no soon after that call. But I actually gained self confidence over the next years while the children were growing up by saying yes to being a leader in 4-H, scouts, Elks wives, choir, a church building committee, a sorority, etc. We were an active family, with skiing, travel, golf, tennis, church, ball games, lifeguarding, dating, dances and sailing on lakes with our Hobe Cat Catamaran. Living at 912 Maple Blvd over eighteen years was filled with growth, happiness, joy and sorrow for our family. In the future I did learn to say, "No" after a lot of accomplishments in the business world but that's another chapter in the story of addresses.

prompt

FAMILIAR ADDRESS:
WRITE A SCENE ASSOCIATED WITH THE ADDRESS

by PHILIP LIBOTT

77 SUNSET STRIP, LOS ANGELES, CA. Already super-bright, and super-warm. Just a hint of a Santa Ana wind, even this far west on Sunset Blvd. The intense light illuminated the surface details of the now shuttered building, which only a few hours before had been the scene of drunken, riotous crowds and loud music. The parking lot was completely empty, except for here and there bits of litter and detritus as souvenirs of the previous night's tumult. This perception, and the sporadic rustling and crinkling of the palm fronds in the quickening breeze, resurrected for me that above, behind, and beneath the facades, freeways, asphalt, concrete, noise and smog of L.A. lived an immutable geographic deity known as California.

FAMILIAR ADDRESS:
WRITE A SCENE ASSOCIATED WITH THE ADDRESS

by RUTH MARCUS

CHAMBERLAIN COURT, Mill Valley, California: A mountain-style A-frame hugs the side of a slope surrounded by a grove of tall eucalyptus trees. The scent is medicinal. When winds funnel over the headlands, the eucalyptus trees engage in a wild dance — swaying and whirling, moaning and groaning. They lean like adolescent athletes doing backbends.

I loved the sound, but it didn't take long to learn that towering eucalyptus trees have shallow-roots. In addition, their branches snap loose becoming harpoons piercing roofs and decks. Nature has a way of making itself known, revealing its beauty, its power and its destructive nature. How similar are we, the human race.

Mapquest Chamberlain Court and you will find it is a short artery off the infamous Highway 1. A short distance further along Highway 1, you come to Muir Woods—a sacred place that I enjoyed for twenty years. I visited in the early morning hours, long before buses of tourists arrived throughout the day. It was one of my favorite places for a meditative walk.

The brilliance of lime against mottled dark green moss covered rocks. The undergrowth, deep duff with unfurling ferns along trickling streams, the sun filtered through a canopy of ancient giant redwoods. The fragrance was intoxicating. The stillness, humbling.

The woods were often wrapped in fog, sometimes a mist— other times a thick cold fog irrigating my nose. I enjoyed the pleasure of the earthen paths before raised boardwalks were built to protect the environment from the bus loads of tourists that visited every year.

Muir Woods was a sacred experience imprinting visceral memories of the importance of silence and the joining with ancient redwoods.

A stark contrast to the silence of Muir Woods: Every Sunday morning, a group of motorcycle riders met at Tam Junction and roared up Highway 1 for a coastal Sunday ride. I imagine these riders loved leaning into the curves, their machines roaring as they wound their way to Stinson Beach. Is it fair to assume their memories are as meaningful as my memories of Muir Woods?

GEOLOGIST / RUMOR GOING AROUND TOWN

by CHERYLE HOSKINS BIGELOW

THERE IS A RUMOR going around town that a geologist unearthed a prehistoric woman: She was wearing an animal skin jacket with shoulder pads and she clutched a spear in one hand and an infant in the other.

prompt

GEOLOGIST / RUMOR GOING AROUND TOWN

by B O N N I E   D I C K M A N N

THERE'S A RUMOR GOING AROUND TOWN that everyone is sitting on a crack. No, not that crack—but a fissure in the surface of the earth right here in Cedar Grove, Washington. I laughed when I first heard the theory. Sure we'd had small tremors, but nothing serious.

Our town council decided to hire a geologist to come check things out and as one of the newer members of the council I was given the job of introducing him to various families that had experienced damage to their homes from our most recent tremors.

No one told me John Martinson would be the total definition of tall, dark and handsome—and single.

We spent the day interviewing the families and at the last appointment were told a sinkhole had appeared two miles down Harrison Lane just off Route 101. On the drive there, we started talking about life and it seemed we had a lot in common.

We arrived at our destination and as I put the car in "Park," John quickly got out and came around to open my door and help me out. As I stood, he leaned down and kissed me and I felt the earth move under my feet.

prompt

GEOLOGIST / RUMOR GOING AROUND TOWN

by D I A N N E   L .   K N O X

STONE

He rocked my world
Like a rumor going around town
This small town
Tongues tumbling, amplifying
With each new telling
Until the pebbles of truth
Gathered into a giant formation
Teetering on the edge of possibility
Then crashing
A geologist the only one
Able to discern the history
Scientifically determining reality
He rocked my world
Rumors were dust to the actual stone.

prompt
GEOLOGIST / RUMOR GOING AROUND TOWN

by PHILIP LIBOTT

SHE WAS FROM off-world, that much we knew about her. As a Federation geologist, she must have been brought in by the Ruling Council to perform a second analysis of the unusual rocks and remains Benford's squad had unearthed, or rather I should say, "unmartianed" late last week at the Pynchon Escarpment, directly NE of the addition. At least, this was the rumor going on throughout the settlement, as quick to catch on as a spreading boron fire would on Cataluga's 5th moon, Jocasta.

By her bearing, her voice, and her mannerisms, Amanda Petersen, a no-nonsense researcher and geologist, would be somebody not to trifle with, someone who would bring a rigorous independence to the investigation, so that the settlement could gain a clearer picture of what some obviously very human remains, thousands of years old, were doing laying in cross-bedded sandstone, on a Martian outcropping in the year 2045.

GEOLOGIST / RUMOR GOING AROUND TOWN

by LILY TODD

EUREKA WAS a small Rocky Mountain town of only 1,100 people. Located fifty miles from a proper town, entertainment was hard to come by. So the local sewing circle came up with a solution. When they met in the basement of the only church every Tuesday and Friday mornings, they joyfully spread the news. The news was the latest rumor going around town which they started.

What fun they had. Miss Wisdom, the 70-year-old librarian, was engaged to the Fuller Brush salesman. Bella La Roe, the gym teacher who liked girls, was pregnant. (Eureka was a modern, well-informed town.) Next Bella was trying to decide if the father was the new postman or the geologist from Salt Lake City. And so the stories came, twice a week.

It's hard to fault these do-gooders for their imagination as they stitch uniforms for the high school band or quilts to be auctioned off as fund raisers.

Soon lines formed on sewing day outside the church. Snoopy people who wanted to be first to know were just strolling by or on their way somewhere.

I tracked these "rumors" over five years. My discovery: the rumors had a seventy-one and a half percent accuracy rate, if you allowed two years for them to materialize. It's surprising how many nineteen month babies these ladies produced.

GOOD MORNING! COCK-A-DOODLE-DOO

by SUSAN GEIS

OUR HOUSE WAS LOCATED out in the country. We owned five acres and most of the other neighbors lived on that many acres or more. Almost everyone had a pasture pet. There were horses, donkeys, goats, sheep, chickens, etc.

We had a wood stove and everyone knows that nothing warms a house as well during the winter months. Being a light sleeper, I would get up in the night, around three or four o-clock, to add a few logs so our house would be toasty warm when we got up to start our day.

We built our house with a door to the outside porch right next to the stove where we stacked wood in a wheelbarrow. It made it easy to feed the stove and keep soot, pieces of wood, bark, and dirt from being tracked across the living room. I would open the outside door, turn on the big bright outside light, get a few logs, throw them in the stove, close the door and turn off the light.

Neighbors who lived due west of us, had chickens and the loudest rooster alive. Neighbors would complain that he was not only the loudest rooster they had ever heard but also the dumbest rooster because he would crow at two, three and even four in the morning. Way before the sun ever came up!

I thought he was the smartest rooster I ever knew!

Every time, no matter what time I got up to load the stove in the early morning hours and turned on that big bright light coming from the east, that rooster would start to crow.

HE DIDN'T UNDERSTAND WHAT HE HAD DONE

by SUSAN GEIS

IT ALL BEGAN when my brother and I decided to spend a week together at the family cabin, on Hood Canal, in beautiful green Washington State.

The cabin was built in the 1960's. It wasn't big or fancy but all of us liked to go there for a great vacation together. Our kids had a wonderful time playing and fishing on the beach. My brother and I lived in different cities, far apart, so the cousins didn't see each other very often.

His kids were older and would be going off to college soon. We knew that this might be the last summer for all of us to get together.

I do understand that the more kids you have in a family, the more lenient you become. My brother, Steve, had three children, two boys and a girl where my husband and I only had the one girl. Older children say how lucky and 'easy' the youngest kid in the family, has it. The parents get beat down and pretty relaxed on rules concerning dating and curfews, and by the time the youngest one comes along things are pretty relaxed. After raising three kids my brother was pretty relaxed.

My husband and I had tried to shield and shelter our daughter from the evil things in life and to keep her as innocent for as long as we could. We did pretty well until that fateful summer, at the cabin, with Uncle Steve.

Yeah, we knew the world held bad things but my brother didn't have the right to expose our daughter to the sins of the world. That was our job, not his!

So…when I walked into the cabin I couldn't believe my older brother was blissfully exposing my darling, 2-year-old daughter, to a sugar drenched, powder coated, cute little marshmallow that you put in hot chocolate.

There he was, putting that tiny cute little marshmallow on her innocent stretched out tongue.

I knew then, that the sacrifices and sheltering we had carefully cultivated ended on that fateful day. There went two years of carefully not introducing my daughter to the evils of sugar, sweets, candy, and whipped cream.

It was all in vain!

The minute she closed her innocent little mouth around that tiny little marshmallow her eyes got huge. They were even sparkling! She said in her amazed little baby marshmallow breath, "What was that?"

I knew then that her sweet innocence was gone forever.

prompt
HE DIDN'T UNDERSTAND WHAT HE HAD DONE

by GEORGE MILLER

HE DIDN'T UNDERSTAND what he'd done when he opened that
envelope, mistakenly left in his box and clearly addressed to his new
neighbors. Curiosity about the new family next door, and his lack of
courtesy and restraint let him open that letter with no more energy
or delay than the blink of an eye. No return address, automated
printing and font—junk mail. They'll never miss it.

He'd tried to glean what he could about his new neighbor family
—a young couple with three young kids. Nosy, but too shy (or rude)
to introduce himself, he made a point of spying on them whenever
he heard the house door open, trying to learn what he could. They'd
actually caught him looking from behind his curtains a few times,
but instead of acknowledging and waving, they quickly turned away
and continued with their business. The last time he'd been caught,
the mother had quickly ushered the kids from the backyard back
into the house, and it seemed the kids had been absent from the yard
for the last week.

Surprisingly, inside the plain, nondescript envelope was a hand
written note, written in terse irregular cursive. There were multiple
exclamation points, lots of underlining and bold lettering, and what
was that stain? Coffee? Blood? In spite of the poor handwriting, it
only took a minute to read.

"I **know** you've seen that guy that lives to your west!!! You've had
a **full month** now—more than you deserve!!!! MARK MY WORD—

if you don't finish our business by this weekend, **you'll be finished too!!** And, just in case you're losing your nerve, take a look in the envelope!!!"

He looked back in the envelope, and there at the bottom was a lock of blond hair.

Oh my God! What is this about? Is this for real, or a joke? I live west of them. This letter is about me...and it's Thursday!

HE DIDN'T UNDERSTAND WHAT HE HAD DONE

by VYKKI MORRISON

HE DIDN'T UNDERSTAND WHAT HE HAD DONE, but it was magnificent.

I stared into a doorway, rendered speechless, my mind boggled. It was obvious to me that his was an incomparable gift. My eyes scanned tables, shelves, the floor. There were hundreds, crammed into and onto every space. Each one exquisitely delicate, every one unique.

"You can touch them" his mother said, coming up behind me. "He doesn't mind."

I didn't know which one to reach for first—which of these marvelous, ethereal clockwork men. My hands lit on a horse and rider facing a woman and set it in motion. I stood transfixed as the horse reared up and the rider lifted his hat with smooth, lifelike movements. The woman inclined her head.

No, he didn't understand what he had done, this autistic boy, but it was magnificent.

prompt
HOW I MAKE MEANING

by GLEN BARBIERI

THINK. WRITE. CALCULATE. Am I using the right equations? Are the numbers right? Recalculate. List. Can't have enough lists. Pages and pages of lists. Lists within lists. Where are those equations? Equations. Time!

HOW I MAKE MEANING

by PHILIP LIBOTT

IF AN EXPERIENCE affects me poignantly and deeply, such that I think about my puppy Snickers, our 7-year-old Mini-Schnauzer we had to put down a year ago because of fast moving cancer in his spleen and liver, then I know that whatever I'm living through right at that moment is significant, and I feel that it has some profound meaning for my life.

HOW I MAKE MEANING

by VYKKI MORRISON

I LOVE TO WRITE, mostly because I love the creative process. I love the way life provides visions, and sounds, scents and substances around us to choose as input. I get to translate that through me. I guess one could say I'm making meaning.

prompt

HE SAID, SHE SAID

by GORDON ANDERSON

THE MEETING

A meeting in a supermarket took place.

"Is that really you…Nadine?"

"What did you say?"

"Is that really you…Nadine?"

"Yes…who are you?"

"I'm Eddy…don't you remember me?"

"Well…maybe."

"I'm Eddy…I use to tease you in the 7th grade…I thought I was in love with you, too."

"Really—Eddy, why didn't you tell me?"

"I was afraid you would not like me."

"Eddy…I had a crush on you, too."

"You did…you really did?"

"Yes—I did."

"That's amazing."

"It's interesting."

"Dear Nadine…it's been ten years…but are you single…I am."

"Yes…I am…Eddy."

"Nadine…would you like to go on a date with me?"

Yes…Eddy—I would love to."

Nadine…that's just great."

They walked into the parking lot together.

HE SAID, SHE SAID

by JUDY LARIMORE

He said: "You can't do that"
She said: "Just watch me"

IMAGINE ALL THE PEOPLE

by JIM WEATHERLY

IMAGINE ALL THE PEOPLE who do not wash their hands.

Or those who spend entirety never traveling beyond their limits.

What about the people who can read, but do not—simply relying on TV for information.

Imagine all the people who have never streaked or skinny-dipped.

Or imagine everyone naked (and twisting and shouting).

Imagine all the people who never scan the entire menu—just ordering the same ol' same ol'...

Or all the people who put up with terrible jobs and tyrant relationships of the heart.

In some ways, when I imagine these things, I am kind of glad the world does not live as one.

prompt

IF IT WEREN'T FOR _____, I WOULD NEVER HAVE _____

by GEORGE MILLER

IF IT WEREN'T FOR the passage of time, I would never have gained a perception of timelessness. If it weren't for an understanding of timelessness, I would never have seen beyond the illusions of lack and want and fear. If it weren't for acknowledging those illusions, I would never have seen that every point of the circle of my life has been both a beginning and an end—each all and nothing. If not for that awareness, I would never have tasted the sweetness of the passage of my time.

IF IT WEREN'T FOR _____, I WOULD NEVER HAVE _____

by LILY TODD

IF IT WEREN'T FOR COOKING, I would never have married.

I hate to cook. Even making instant coffee created a lasting black mark on my day.

When I met Lee, I was intrigued. He was consumed by food, great food, gourmet food.

On our first date we had a lobster for an appetizer, four full meal orders each different that we shared and a sampling of five high calorie desserts each. The man was ecstatic when I matched him bite for bite. After three days of Ritz crackers, I was famished.

His eyes glowed as he laid out the future:

In the fall, sweet Bing cherries from Flathead Lake in Montana, summer corn in Yakima, lobster season caused a trip to New England, coffee harvest in Columbia (the country), chocolates mean France, pineapples called for an excursion to Hawaii and so on.

If it wasn't for cooking, I would never have married. Now I weigh 374 pounds. Why didn't I just learn to cook?

by TRUDY MCFARLAND

THE OLD CARPENTER stood back looking at the large, white chunk of wood. It was massive and heavy. The wood smelled of pine and forest. He loved that smell. His wrinkled and calloused hands stroked the large piece of wood and his old eyes surveyed it. He gazed at it in awe. In all his years he had never seen or used such a piece of wood in any of his projects.

The old carpenter picked up a chisel and began to work. Minutes, hours, days later and he had barely chiseled away any of the enormous chunk of wood. It was a beast, a large wild animal, waiting to be tamed by his old gnarled hands. His work continued for weeks. What emerged surprised even him, a Nativity, so beautiful and beyond compare to any other Nativity. The lines of the wood were perfect in every detail, all one piece, yet many intricate parts. Mary, Joseph and the baby Jesus were so flawless, each a perfectly chiseled part of the wood. The Nativity seemed to glow with the carpenter's life and spirit he had so lovingly carved into the wood. It was his last work of art for the old carpenter died that night, Christmas Eve. It was his crowning piece of glory, a work of pure love. For years to come the Nativity would bring awe and wonder to all who beheld it's beauty.

by PATRICIA DEMARCO

IF CAUGHT, the stolen goods list would read: three short pencils and three empty donation envelopes.

Penelope purloined said items from the offering tray after making sure her position was directly behind a woman with long, thick wavy hair which draped over the pew's back and cascaded over the small offering's shelf in front of Penelope, thereby naturally hiding it from view.

Carefully placing a pencil into each envelope along with two, one-dollar bills, a folded notecard and a USPS Forever Stamp, she laid them inside her personal bible. Then she took a fourth donation envelope and placed into it a handful of coin found at the bottom of her purse, holding the small manila envelope up in plain sight of the other parishioners.

The minister announced the brothers were to pass the collection plate around and would the congregation please dig deep and be generous. "Sorry, Pastor," she mumbled under her breath as the plate came her way. "You'll understand. The homeless on the steps outside the church need encouragement and this offering, too."

MINISTER / STOLEN GOODS

by JIM WEATHERLY

I HAVE LEARNED over the years that I am my own minister. That my stolen goods, my spirituality, are deeper than the sunken tub I was prodded into at such an elementary age. Dunked in salty, icy water that made me speak in tongues when I surfaced.

My pulpit is the forest. There, I walk slowly and delicately between fallen limbs and evergreen dew. Listening in the quiet and open space for Desert Fathers to fill my chest and lungs with lessons I missed before. To find a rock or trunk to nestle with and scroll the sermons Sunday school failed to execute accordingly.

The stream is my wine. A peanut butter sandwich my bread. I close my eyes and hear a choir of birds and branches. I am replenished. I am still good. I am my own minister.

prompt

MOUNTAIN TOP / STAIN / TELEPHONE

by PATRICIA DEMARCO

THE TELEPHONE RINGS. I hesitate and check the number prompt. Not a number I knew or a business I shopped at.

"Oh, well. If they think it's that important, they'll leave a message." I stare out the window at the majestic scene in front of me, a ridge of mountaintops pushed up millennia ago and now covered with snowfields and glaciers warming to the sun's embrace.

I look at the prompt ready to push "view" on the menu when the phone buzzes that a message, indeed, has been recorded.

I'm not a talker and my friends know I'd prefer an e-mail or slow mail correspondence than use a phone. Don't bother to say the word Skype and as for answering cell phones as I drive, forget it!! Tracing my reluctant attitude, it comes from being the daughter of an over-worked, and only local telephone lineman in the county over sixty years ago. I was expected to answer the party-line phone and fabricate tales of why he couldn't be reached even though he was sitting or lying down across the room. Dad just couldn't say "No, I'm too tired to come out or it's just too dangerous right now in this weather!" because he had a family to feed so the rest of us had to figure out the "Why" for him. I have a low trust level for authenticity when it comes to phone conversations.

I press the "Voice Mail" and an unfamiliar voice chimes in, overly exuberant for this early in the morning. It becomes clear that this message is for someone else but I can't draw myself away. Her life is far more interesting than mine.

I grab my coffee cup which flies out of my hand and onto the white linen tablecloth, leaving a swath of coffee stain which in an instant of artistic insight, reminds me of a bouquet of dried, brown autumn foliage....(to eventually be continued.)

by TERRY MOORE

IT WAS 3 A.M. when the phone rang. Unusual to say the least. I'm at the end of a 40-mile long access road to a forest fire lookout station on the top of Black Elk Mountain. I answered the phone and immediately heard the voice of Chief Ranger Thornby. As I became more awake, I came to understand that the fire on the north side of my mountain had changed direction, and that I should expedite getting out of here.

It took me all of three minutes to gather up my stuff and another two to climb down to the Jeep, and to gauge the glow of the fire for speed and direction. I should, I thought, be able to drive out ahead of the flames, just barely. The access road to the tower was accessible by four wheel drive only, and in my panicked hurry, there would be plenty of inspiration for fouling my pants.

by VYKKI MORRISON

CLEANING BUCKET beside her, she stoops to reach for supplies. Her withered hands shake, her body is bowed. She is tired, she is worried, and her heart aches, but life goes on.

She is passing time by thoroughly cleaning an already spotless house. As she sprays, one ear listens for the car that will bring her to his deathbed. As she scrubs, tears run down her face, salting soapy water. She wrings the cloth and wipes down a wooden window sash in the mountaintop home they've shared for seventy-five years. It is already clean.

She is far away in a midnight dance, head on shoulder, hand in hand, when the telephone rings. She doesn't hear it at first, only slowly recognizing its refrain of death. The dance ends; she drops to her knees and scrubs at the stain her tears make.

prompt

MOUNTAIN TOP / STAIN / TELEPHONE

by LILY TODD

I LOVED. I LOST. Here I sit on the edge of the world it seems. It's just our private mountain top as we always called it, located only five and a half miles from home, or what used to be our home. It was our home until Judith moved into town.

So, here I am. Seventeen years ago, we had our first date here. Right there, under the stunted fir tree. A picnic, KFC chicken, grapes and a $1.98 bottle of wine. A gourmet feast, I said, with the prettiest girl in town.

As we dined, we promised each other to keep this place sacred and only speak the truth here.

Judith moved in with her lover three days, fourteen hours and six minutes ago.

I left a message yesterday saying I would be here at noon, the exact time of our first visit. I asked her to come or call if she still had any feelings for me. "If you don't, you won't be bothered by your husband again," I said.

I watched the sun rise and send the shadows away on this, our mountain top. I watched the hands move to noon on my watch. I watched the minute hand slowly move past, one minute, two minutes, three minutes.

At five past, I stood up and unhurriedly took a step forward, a big step, the start of the drop which will leave a stain on the rocks far below. From my pocket, I heard the telephone ring.

MY MOTHER NEVER____

by CHERYLE HOSKINS BIGELOW

MY MOTHER NEVER audited the truth of her words. If she said it was fifty cents, it was a dollar.

My Mother always said "Don't worry about what other people think" and my Mother never did.

My Mother lived until she was ninety-five years old and my Mother never quit dispensing controversial, irreverent and practical advice.

by RUTH MARCUS

THE SOUND OF BROKEN GLASS pierced the morning silence. I sat up with a start. First light cast a blue streak along the north wall of my bedroom. My Golden Lab took a stand, his nose in the air, a baritone woof-woof familiar to my ears as he warned me of danger.

I confess, his bark seldom turned up any danger, but I pulled on my robe and slippers, opened the bedroom door with hesitation as he pushed his way past me and quick-trotted down the hall, down the stairs—his toe nails clickity-clacking as he descended. I was reminded it was time to cut his nails.

It was only 5:15 a.m. What was happening to cause the sound of broken glass? My heart rate increased as the thought of an intruder rushed through my mind. Here I am, navigating the stairs in the dark. What was I going to do if I confronted a burglar? Petey-dog continued his bark as he skidded around the corner into the kitchen.

His barking came to a sudden halt. A whimpering sound followed. "What on earth?" my mind questioned as I turned on the kitchen light. Their on the kitchen floor, a wounded gull.

ONE BROKEN WINDOW

by TRUDY MCFARLAND

The sound of breaking glass pierces the air.
He stands in shock.
Did I really just do that?
Run!
His feet begin to move.
No!
He has to tell someone.
He hears voices and shouting.
Hey! Who broke my window?
He starts to run but his heart tells him no. He has to make this right.
His feet feel like heavy stones, like mud is caked all over them.
He is fighting a battle inside.
Should he tell or should he run?
The voices are getting louder.
Who broke my window? Did you? Did you?
The woman is getting closer to him. She spots him and their eyes meet.
His heart jumps into his throat and he can't speak. Tears begin to course down his cheeks in embarrassment and shame.
Then something unexpected, the woman smiles.
He is confused. He tries to speak again but no words come out.

His mouth is dry but his cheeks are wet.

The woman smiles again and as she reaches him, she takes his hand, still smiling.

She says it's okay.

Confused, the boy finally manages to speak, it's okay?

The woman says, yes, it's okay; I never liked that window anyway. It's just one broken window.

He stands in shock and then he smiles too.

Come inside says the woman. It's hot out here and I'll give you some lemonade.

We'll listen to the birds sing and feel the breeze through the beautiful, new hole in my house.

ONE OF THE GREATEST SURPRISES IN MY LIFE

by BONNIE DICKMANN

AS A CHILD, I grew up in a religious family and was raised to believe a masculine God was to be worshipped as our Creator and the Supreme Being. One of the greatest surprises in my adult life came when I realized it is Mother Nature who is at the core of my belief in a Creator.

I spent my life as a stay-at-home mother and I find it is the female entity who best fits any description of love, selflessness and nurturing.

Look deep into nature and find all that is beautiful and right. In the verdant green of a rain forest, the colors of butterflies, birds and flowers are what convince me there is a supreme power of some sort working magic in feathers and foliage.

Could a male figure possibly put together the vibrant red, green and yellow of a scarlet macaw and have it work? Could he make the ocean a color of blue never found in a box of sixty-five crayons or produce a waterfall path for a river gliding through a jungle to the ocean?

No—I think not. And that's why I believe in Mother Nature. I believe in her ability to give life and color to this world. I also believe in her innate sense as to when life should cease on this earthy plane and move on to another dimension.

ONE OF THE HARDEST DECISIONS I'VE EVER HAD TO MAKE

by G E O R G E   M I L L E R

ONE OF THE HARDEST decisions I've ever had to make was not a specific decision, but a choice to take action, to step, to take initiative, to choose and act based on my own beliefs, my intentions, and to hold and honor them as my responsibilities in making my place in the world.

ONE OF THE HARDEST DECISIONS I'VE EVER HAD TO MAKE

by TERRY MOORE

ONE OF THE HARDEST decisions I ever had to make involved a Piper Cub aircraft, an airstrip on a mountain top, and an injured miner.

I was enroute from Ketchikan to Johnson's Island, and had been airborne for about an hour, when I received a call from air traffic. Jake, the caller asked, can you divert to the dirt strip on Jergen's mountain. We need a medevac for an injured miner, he said. I agreed to do it, as I happened to have a rare empty seat.

I had been in and out of that strip about five times. I didn't like the strip. You had to land going uphill...

ONE SOUND

by DIANNE L. KNOX

CLICK

Key turned in the lock
She came through the door
Put her purse on the hall table
Took off her coat and shoes
Home is the place
She has been longing for all day
Quiet calming protective walls
Against hectic fury bustling bodies.

by GORDON ANDERSON

THANKSGIVING NAPKINS

TRYING TOO HARD isn't easy when you don't know what you are doing in the first place. Like gee whiz…I'm a growing outdoor boy. I'm with my Mom trying to help her set the Thanksgiving Table—from the fancy white linen table cloth on down to every crystal glass, Noritake China plate and silver knife, fork, and spoon.

I'm nearing seven years old and the oldest kid in the family. My brother and sister are still little kids and too young to help set the table. I am a big boy now, and I am to learn and set the table with my mother. I would much rather be outside catching and passing my football around with some neighbor kids. But Thanksgiving is nice and celebratory…I think that's the word for having a good time and getting together to pork out on turkey and mashed potatoes and gravy. Anyway my Mom and I put the dining table leaves in and then spread out the large Thanksgiving tablecloth over the now very large and long table as my little brother and sister stand by and watch. Twelve people can sit at our now banquet table with the two table leaves in place.

After getting the table cloth in place came the dozen-ironed linen napkins, and I was to get them and put each one of them down in its proper position. Well, I wanted my orange juice first, so I went to the refrigerator, we called it the fridge, and got me a glass full of orange juice, and then I went to the kitchen nook table. I picked up and clutched the dozen-ironed linen napkins in my hands along with my near full glass of orange juice. I guess I was in a hurry to get done—that's why I got everything at once, and I headed for the dining room table. I tripped on the rug's edge, dropped all of the napkins, and my glass of orange juice fell breaking into pieces and spilling sticky orange juice over most every linen napkin. I wound up on the floor but I did not get cut and no one got hurt. My younger sister thought it was funny and laughed, and my little brother cried. My Mom stood there a moment flushed with her hands on her hips. And then I helped her sweep up the broken glass pieces, pick up all the soppy napkins and spot mop the floor. I felt bad and embarrassed.

Anyway, Mom sat me down at the kitchen nook table and brought a stack of paper napkins. She sat down with me and taught me how to fold and make a fancy fan out of a paper napkin. Then she had me fold and make all of the rest. She had me meet her approval of each one as I finished. I counted eighteen when I had finished folding them all. Next Mom showed me how she wanted the napkins placed at each table setting. The six extra fan napkins were stacked and set on a plate on the china hutch. My mother and I patiently set the Thanksgiving table with all the China plates, saucers and cups, and crystal glassware, and silverware in their proper position.

Then Mom brought out the centerpiece, which was a small bouquet of flowers with three candles. Mom handed me the matchbox and let me light all three candles. Lighting the candles made me feel good. She put her arms around me and gave me a hug and said, "Thanks for helping me set the table…those paper fan napkins…all in their place look real, real nice."

Then she marched me in the kitchen where my sister and brother were sitting, and I sat down on the bench in front of a large glass of orange juice and a plate of just fresh baked chocolate-chip cookies.

PARADE / MISTAKE / LUNCH

by TERRY MOORE

THERE WAS A CONSTANT stream of customers parading in and out of the restaurant. A blue neon sign identified the place as "Sparkies."

I had never visited this restaurant before and my curiosity was piqued. A dozen steps later, and I was greeted with some delicious aromas. That sealed the deal and pushed me past my desire to get home early. Inside, I was greeted by the babble of contented sounding voices, scurrying waiters, and starched white tablecloths.

A sweet young waitress guided me to a window table, handed me a menu, and scurried away with a reminder that she would be right back. I took off my jacket and hung it on an ornate brass coat hook on the wall next to the table. I sat down, noted that there was a nice view of the harbor, and opened the menu to see what delights awaited. There was a note paper-clipped inside the menu. "Get out quickly," the note said. "I'll meet you on the corner. Lunch here is a mistake."

PARANOID (YOU THINK I'M PARANOID?)

by CHERYLE HOSKINS BIGELOW

"DON'T WORRY so much", he said. "We will handle it when it happens." Why anticipate, why prepare, why look for the emergency exit I wondered.

He thinks the missile, the earthquake, the volcano, the robber, will bother our neighbors but we will be just fine. Does he mean as long as his favorite coffee shop survives the "end of times" so he can order a peanut butter-flavored mocha?

PARANOID (YOU THINK I'M PARANOID?)

by DIANNE L. KNOX

NOIDS

What are you looking at
What do you mean by that
Why are you saying that to me
Quit picking on me
They keep following me
That pair over there
You think life is hard for you
Pitfalls hard to avoid
Crises at every turn
And you think I'm paranoid.

PARANOID (YOU THINK I'M PARANOID?)

by PHILIP LIBOTT

I'VE MADE THE MISTAKE before of thinking that I had the job, and would receive a call any day to be scheduled for an interview that was just a formality. Then, I'd wind up never hearing back at all from the employer! I know that I have all the qualifications for the job, but something's nagging at me and deflating my self-esteem. Do you think I'm just being paranoid about this one?

I didn't leave my last job under the best of circumstances. The letter that I emailed to my boss, Dan Summers just before I was "laid off," in which I wrote critically about the lack of completeness of the equipment caches at the outstations, probably didn't win me any accolades from management. As much as I want to believe that this prospective employer should consider me only on the merits of my most recent work experience, and should be looking at the positive results our team accomplished using the new methods and equipment, I'm afraid that if they talk to Dan, he'll probably give me a bad reference, just because I criticized my prior employer's commitment to their (our) outlying sites! Oh, hell, I'm probably just being paranoid, don't you think?

PEOPLE WHO CHALLENGE ME

by CHERYLE HOSKINS BIGELOW

MY HUSBAND asked, "Have you seen my fig bar?"
I replied, "They are in the pantry."
"No," he said, "I mean the one I was eating."

PHONE CALL INTERRUPTED

by BONNIE DICKMANN

SHOULD I CALL HIM?

The photo in the paper triggered memories from so long ago. She remembered it as a time of youthful innocence with hopes for a future.

Should I? No! Leave it alone. You don't need to go through that again.

But that photo—it brought back so many memories. Her hand hovered over the receiver. Damn!

She picked it up and punched in the numbers—one ring, two, three.

"Hello?" His deep voice hadn't changed in fifteen years.

"Hello Richard."

"Diane—you saw it. I knew you'd call!"

With that Mary Ann hung up.

QUIRKY FAMILY MEMBER

by GEORGE MILLER

HE'S ALMOST MY physical opposite, tall and lumbering, a true bear in all but temperament, powerful in ways I'll never be. Yet, we are so alike in spite of the size difference, and have carried a strong cousin bond all our lives. Born in the same year, good natured, generally, and we both strive to uplift ourselves and those around us. We both often place ourselves last in so many ways and processes. We've both developed love and a kinship with nature that in many ways is much stronger and durable than what we each hold with society and, often, even family. God, he's a quirky guy.

RELUCTANTLY, HE HANDED OVER THE KEY

by GEORGE MILLER

RELUCTANTLY, he handed over the key to his steady, dependable, old friend, the '55 Dodge Power Wagon, his business partner, and buddy through 40 years, three engine rebuilds, and 167 new home completions. They'd seen some good times together.

He felt a little guilty trading his mainstay until he looked, again over to the flashy, cherry-red showroom beauty he'd been scoping for the last three months. Today was the day he'd step into his new life—treating himself for once. He took the new key and started toward his new baby, to his new self, feeling his aches, pain, and age literally falling away, then...he stopped.

After a moment, he realized he wasn't moving to a new, better life, but was actually throwing himself and his whole life away.

He turned around, handed the Tesla key back to the young salesgirl, took back his smooth, familiar, still warm Dodge key—and his life—and walked out the showroom door with a long-missed spring in his old step.

RELUCTANTLY, HE HANDED OVER THE KEY

by VYKKI MORRISON

RELUCTANTLY, he handed over the key. "Ijustwantedtoseewhat wasinside," Adam mumbled, words running together.

"You seem to have figured it out pretty quickly, young man," replied the shopkeeper sternly.

"Exactly how did you get the key?"

"I found the key," he said, defiantly. "It was just sitting there on the rack." He took a deep breath and rushed on. "Sarah told me about the elves back there making everything. I wanted to see the magic. I just wanted to see."

"And were there elves?"

"No," said Adam. "They musta already finished and gone home." He stared at the floor, then raised his head to the shopkeeper earnestly.

"But I didn't touch anything, I promise," said the voice of innocence. A chocolate-smeared face looked straight at him. The chocolatier smiled, a little magic dribbling from his fingertips.

SHE SHOULD HAVE BEEN HOME HOURS AGO

by BONNIE DICKMANN

WHY DO I ALWAYS end up waiting for her? No text, no call. I just sit here, worried sick, and wait. This is the most inconsiderate thing a woman can do to her husband. I'm going to let her know that when she finally gets home.

I've never raised my hand to her, but now I don't know why. Tonight could be a first in that department. Doesn't she ever consider my feelings? She must know after thirty years of marriage, how much I worry about her going out at night with that rowdy bunch of bridge players. They drink so darn much coffee they all start babbling on and on and I'll bet no one bothers to look at a clock.

Wait. Is that her key in the lock? Boy now she's gonna get it!

Carol walks in the room and he leaps out of his chair and wraps her in a loving embrace.

"Honey, I'm so glad you're finally home. I was so worried."

"Dan, it's only 8:30. I'm always home before 9:00."

SHE SHOULD HAVE BEEN HOME HOURS AGO

by PHILIP LIBOTT

SHE SHOULD HAVE been home hours ago. I was waiting for my teenaged daughter to get off her shift at the Dairy Queen, her first job, miles from our home in Sequim. She had moved to Redmond from Sequim, and shared, with six other people, a two-bedroom apartment that was located directly across a busy highway from Microsoft's front gate. She had to move out, quickly, and I'd driven the 1989 four-speed Toyota Pickup with the decrepit canopy—one busted-out window that I'd attempted to seal up with cardboard and duct tape to keep out the rain—all the way out there from Sequim. Trying to make conversation with three computer/tech/nerdy guys in their late teens and early twenties while time dragged by. One of the guys helped me to get the twin bed down from the second-floor apartment and out to the truck. There just wasn't any way that I could fit the box spring, the mattress, and all the rest of my daughter's stuff into the bed of the truck. I'd have to leave the box spring next to the apartment complex's dumpster. I still think about it as such a waste, as the twin box spring and mattress was the single bed I'd bought, as a newly divorced man, almost twenty years earlier, before I'd gotten into the new relationship with a woman who at the time had a 2-year-old daughter.

SHE SHOULD HAVE BEEN HOME HOURS AGO

by VYKKI MORRISON

SHE SHOULD HAVE been home hours ago. A lot longer than that if he were honest. A week. Almost a week this time. Didn't she know he'd be waiting? Where was her reason? He questioned himself, annoyed.

She knew he'd be waiting. Everywhere he looked, every day he looked, it was the same. Dishes in the sink, crumbs on the counters. Casseroles in the fridge, dust on the floor.

It was a holy mess. She'd never think of leaving any type of mess in her pristine home, much less a holy mess. He had his suspicions, but he wanted it fixed.

What was she trying to tell him, he already knew. 'She wants me to let her go. To give her freedom.' After forty years together, this was her newest way of not-saying it. Little trips away, less contact. She'd been distant this past year and it wasn't as though she hadn't mentioned going away once or twice.

'This time she's telling me by making things uncomfortable so that I won't want her here anymore." He felt hurt, pain welling up. 'Doesn't she know I'll always want her?"

"But I'll do it," he decided, looking around. "I'll do it if that will make her happy. I'll ask for a divorce when she comes back this time. Because she loves me. Because, even with the leaving, and the mess, she made sure there were casseroles in the freezer and flowers delivered. How she loved flowers, everywhere!"

He touched each bouquet lovingly, carefully avoiding the condolence cards.

by GORDON ANDERSON

Gun	he drew his gun and fired
Dead	the man fell dead on the floor
Homicide	a justifiable homicide or no?
Wife	his wife sobbed tears
Lawyers	defense and prosecuting attorneys came
Trial	the trial began.

And a follow-up emotional poem:
Upset
he turned the color of high blood pressure red
it happened when the robber came back
when he pulled the trigger and shot him dead
then everything sounded like the end of the world
the trial was set and he felt like burning hell
and very, very upset.

by VYKKI MORRISON

#1
Huge demon, fiery pit, shoulda known.

#2
Put down that giraffe right now!

prompt
SIX WORD NOVEL

by LILY TODD

I do
I did
Now what?

by GEORGE MILLER

IT WAS A SMALL green suitcase, hardly more in size and protection than a cardboard shirt box, now all but collapsed under the weight of fallen timbers and the avalanche of kudzu covering his long abandoned childhood home and all its buried memories. The faded, rotted canvas covering had all but dusted away, and its one broken latch and cracked tan plastic handle were about all it had to brag about. But, that shabby, aged exterior belied the treasures within— many photographs, some he knew to be easily over a hundred years old, letters, school report cards, odd coins from all over the world. And there, the most prized, an old tape recording of voices long passed, still sheltered in the tiny tape player. On a whim, he pressed the switch, and miracle of miracles, it still played. As he listened, lessons and well-wishes peeled away the sadness and those many long years.

by DIANNE L. KNOX

KITA

He leans in
Gets closer than possible
Fur is all that separates
His skin from mine
He nudges my left arm
Toothbrush in my right
Nudges again if I stop
Stroking his ears, thighs, belly
Our morning ritual
Bringing us closer
After the night
We just spent.

SNAPSHOT OF SOMETHING FUNNY OR QUIRKY

by PHILIP LIBOTT

A SUDDEN, STEEP RISE on the mostly flat plain. As Snickers and I followed the well-worn trail closer to this anomaly, we could see that a single tree grew right out of the top of the crag, and that three layers of stones had been placed around the gnarled roots of the tree's base to create a small enclosure, like a corral or a fort. There also was a short plank that had been set on top of two rocks, creating a bench (or an altar?). No one seemed to be around, and a late August wind rustled through the leaves of the tree. As my 7-year-old Mini-Schnauzer and I made our way carefully up onto the rocks and entwined roots of this sacred place, we saw discarded candy and peanut butter cracker wrappers interspersed within the dirt, as though they were offerings to some Sequim spirit. With our eyes and minds cast resolutely downward to investigate the minutiae of the ground, the hawk's sudden piercing scream directly above us in the air over our heads startled both of us. And a man materialized, as if from another, unseen dimension of the very space we were in, holding in one hand a notebook containing detailed sketches of the hawk, and in the other a bag of chicken jerky dog treats.

by RUTH MARCUS

LYDIA STOOD IN FRONT of the floor-to-ceiling mirror in the Fairmont Hotel. She fluffed her hair, pouched her lips as if to kiss herself and unbuttoned her blouse. She eased the sleeves down her shoulders and let the blue blouse slide to the floor. Then, she unbuttoned her slacks and let them pool at her feet. She wore no underwear. Stepping out of her black leather slip-on shoes she strutted toward the concierge's desk in the middle of the lobby.

Two Japanese tourists stared as if shocked, then stared at each other with hands covering their mouths.

Lydia's husband was working the concierge desk. His eyes were focused downward, intent on making a list of things he planned to say to his wife that evening when he returned home. Things having to do with her recent diagnosis of dementia.

As Lydia reached his desk, she made a clicking sound through the left side of her mouth. With her back turned to Carl, she bent over, her naked butt in the air, and farted a series of sputtering pops— then stood up and quick-stepped to her clothes. She pulled on her pants, slipped into the blouse and stepped into her shoes, strutting past Carl, swishing her hips like she imagined a street-walker might do, then exited using the revolving door.

The Japanese tourists turned toward the reservation counter. Carl, in shock, fumbled with a stack of brochures on his desk.

**SOMETHING INTERESTING OR SPECIAL
ABOUT A FAMILY MEMBER OR FRIEND**

by BONNIE DICKMANN

The shadow of your smile
As that raspy laugh
Escaped your lips.

The shadow of your hair
After I gave you the "chemo" cut.
You wanted control over going bald.

The shadow of your body
Thin, tough as nails
Ravaged by the sin of cigarettes.

The shadow of your memory
Nancy—my best friend
The weight of that shadow stays on my heart.

by COLIN SELLWOOD

SHE SAID THAT I SAID THAT YOU SAID.

I WAS HURRYING toward the bus stop, my excitement growing with every step. It was Saturday, and a yellow number seven was due to arrive at any moment and carry me to the soccer ground where our local team would soon be playing against one of the big clubs from up north.

My mind was filled with questions: had our team's captain recovered from the injury he'd suffered last Saturday? Could our best goalscorer rediscover the form that he'd recently lost? Would our famous opponents be stiff and cramped after their four-hour bus ride, or would they be rested and raring to go?

Lost in thought, I didn't notice the two girls walking toward me until I heard one say to the other, "She said that I said that you said." By the time the words had registered in my brain, the girls had passed me by and were out of earshot. Stunned, I paused in mid-stride while they echoed in my head, and I wondered what complicated chain of events could have caused her to say them. For just a moment I thought about asking the girls, but then realized that they were older, maybe thirteen or fourteen, and that I would probably get an earful for being so cheeky, and maybe even a smack around that same ear.

The bus pulled up at that very moment so, still shaking my head, I climbed on board and went upstairs to sit with a group of game-bound friends. During the ride, the girl's words came back to me and

I turned them over in my mind one more time, but was still unable to imagine a situation that involved such complexity.

But then it was forgotten because we were there! Bouncing off the bus, we joined the throngs of supporters making their way down the hedge-lined avenue towards the stadium, singing snatches of songs, waving our team scarves and clapping and chanting as we went. Now, many years later, I don't even remember who won, but as I climbed into bed that night, the girl's words came back to me and I puzzled over them once more, "She said that I said that you said."

Since then, I've mentioned it to a few people. My wife and our two daughters, bless their cotton socks, immediately replied, "Sure, I can understand a girl saying that," and other women have all felt the same way. I've told the story to only a very few men, who all looked at me with blank stares and then changed the subject. Sometimes in quiet moments I'll revisit that day and turn the words over in my head again, but I still can't conceive of any set of circumstances that would require saying, "She said that I said that you said." Of course, in my younger days I did play a lot of soccer which required frequent heading of heavy, wet soccer balls, and I've also drunk my share of after-game beers, so I'm perhaps not the best of judges.

prompt
TALKING DOG / GUEST

by PHILIP LIBOTT

HE WAS AN UNEXPECTED guest on our back deck, a raccoon, nose right up against the screen door of the open sliding door. Our puppy, Snickers, had never encountered any creature like this, and the vocalizations that were coming out of his mouth were like no utterances we had ever heard from our dog. The feral animal, a swirl of black, brown, and gray, moved his head sideways, back and forth, back and forth as if he/she was attempting to mesmerize the Mini-Schnauzer to get him to slide open the screen door, so that he could come in and share the kibble in the metal bowl on the floor by the kitchen table.

prompt

TALKING DOG / GUEST

by LILY TODD

REX KEPT IT a secret. Everyone wondered how he could write such intelligent exposés about current events in Brookside. Brookside was a small college town with a curriculum for creating top international lawyers. A law degree from here guaranteed excellent pay and the pick of foreign assignments.

Rex wrote for the local paper called Brookside Babble. Its circulation exceeded New York Times and was read world-wide. Alumni kept their subscriptions for life.

As long as Buddy lived, Rex was guaranteed everything he ever wanted.

One day Miss Maple came as he was gathering data for the next day's column. Rex did not welcome guests, especially snoopy old spinsters.

"Shut up, Buddy," Rex hissed. But Buddy was an old dog and he kept talking.

"A talking dog," Miss Maple exclaimed. "That's how you get your scoops!"

"If I can use him, I'll keep your secret," she said. "I need to check out my heirs. I think one of them is trying to kill me."

by CHERYLE HOSKINS BIGELOW

I APOLOGIZED to my grown daughters for the sacrifices they made, without their permission, because I carried a briefcase to the office instead of a purse to the PTA.

prompt
THE APOLOGY

by PHILIP LIBOTT

I SAID I WAS SORRY so many times that I eventually felt how hollowed-out and superficial the phrase was sounding. She claimed that it really wasn't my fault, that she had some hand in her own troubles that I was never privy to, and that it was somehow presumptuous of me to take all the blame onto myself. Of course, I thought, if I had sounded the alarm beforehand, and had warned her of the possible disastrous consequences of having this surgical procedure done, she probably wouldn't have listened to me anyway.

THE BIGGEST QUESTION

by TERRY MOORE

WHY ARE WE HERE? Are we a cosmic goof, or a side effect of God's tinkering with the universe? Did another divinity, in a fit of anger, throw a handful of planets like a curve ball thrown by a petulant pitcher in baseball game?

It occurs to me that why we are here is not nearly so important as the fact that we are here, and that mankind has been carefully crafted by thousands or millions of years by whatever forces interact in our environment. It was a stroke of good fortune that all that was necessary to maintain all forms of life was present in the right amounts, at the right time.

The biggest question now is, is the human race too dumb to live, and will it kill itself off, and take a number of other species with it? The biggest answer is, I don't know, but I am glad to have existed. The next biggest mystery? Is there anything after?

THE MOST INTERESTING PERSON IN MY FAMILY

by HEIDI HANSEN

WITHOUT A DOUBT my Uncle Jack is the most interesting person in my family. He'd show up all of a sudden, unplanned, uninvited and he'd bring a gift—sometimes it was a bottle of scotch for my dad, once a black lab puppy, and at my wedding, a clock he claimed to have brought back from overseas. The clock was a huge squat piece of oak that took up most of the mantel, but never ran. I had a clock repair person over to try and tune it, but after three hours, he shook his head and declared it impossible. This company, he said, never did turn out a good clock. Then I learned it was built in Tennessee and the clock company was out of business.

Uncle Jack told great stories and usually held an audience for hours. They'd come in close as his voice dropped to a whisper, then laugh heartedly at his punchline.

Uncle Jack never married nor fathered any children for all we knew. There were years missing in his resume. One cousin said that he'd been put in jail for bouncing checks, another said he worked with the mob in Las Vegas.

At one time, he sold cars; not a specific make or model, but the unusual or those once owned by celebrities. Once he came in a silver Rolls Royce and claimed a long list of Hollywood actors had owned or driven in the car.

As I grew up, I took him less at his word and made sure when he showed up to lock up any valuables I had. No one ever said he stole things but things went missing without explanation when Uncle Jack visited. Difficult to say that it was Uncle Jack but usually there was a houseful of relatives at the time of his visits.

My father liked the story of Uncle Jack coming to a Thanksgiving dinner dressed in a naval uniform. He claimed to be serving but a year later he showed up dressed in army fatigues.

THE MOST INTERESTING PERSON IN MY FAMILY

by JUDY LARIMORE

THE MOST INTERESTING person in my family would have to be my 49-year-old son, Dave. He has always been creative. At six years old on a trip to the Oklahoma City Zoo, he wanted to take a photo of a bear using my Nikon camera. As he balanced it on an iron railing, he adjusted the zoom and held it still while he clicked the shutter. I helped him develop it in the darkroom where I taught a 4-H group. When I saw how good it turned out, I encouraged him to enter it in the local fair. As we entered the building, I told him not to be discouraged if it didn't win a ribbon. To my surprise it won the best ribbon. A reporter was there and took a photo of us. The caption in the paper said, "Six year old beats his mother and others at the fair with a grand championship ribbon of his photo of a bear."

He has always marched to his own drummer. I remember the time he was eight. I came home to find he had taken the doors off of his step in closet. He had removed the sliding closet doors and his clothes were nowhere in sight.

When I walked in I saw him sitting in his new "Man Cave." That term hadn't been invented in the seventies, but that is what it was. There he sat in his folding canvas chair, the one he used when we went camping and sailing with the catamaran. Now it was used to watch the TV he had placed on a stand in front of his chair.

I asked, "Dave where are your clothes?"

"In my drawers Mom."

I looked and said, "Dave this isn't all of them, where are the rest of your clothes?"

He hesitated for a while and then said, "They are under my bed."

I let him use his man cave for a while where he practiced his singing and watched his favorite TV shows.

After high school Dave followed in my footsteps, making a move to California. Earlier my twenty-year marriage in Kansas had ended and I had moved to the west coast. Enrolling in San Jose State University, he received a degree in art. He again marched to his own drummer when one of his professors wanted to buy one of his abstract paintings.

"No, I don't want to sell it," he said.

"Why not?" I asked.

"Because Mom, I like to look at them from time to time and make changes."

One day I said, "Dave, most of your paintings are really bright colors but my favorite is that pastel painting."

"Maybe one day, Mom, I'll give it to you."

Many times he turned down offers to buy paintings. I think they were like his offspring, each one irreplaceable. Showing them in an exhibit was OK but they came back home with him. After college graduation, he chose to live in a huge warehouse in downtown San Jose where he could play the music he composed on the piano and listen to recorded music as loud as he wanted to. That huge building provided the space to create paintings ten feet by eight feet and larger. There are over one hundred of them.

When the city of San Jose decided to tear down the warehouse to make a parking lot, they offered Dave $5,000 to move.

I said, "What are you going to do?"

His answer, "Find another warehouse."

Moving his paintings was a massive job since he was on the top floor of three stories. My son is creative and found treasures in discarded items in the alleyway behind the warehouse, some to use in his paintings. He had room to be a hoarder in the warehouse and this also added to the overwhelming move from one warehouse to another. To this day he can't resist free items on Craigslist to use in his art.

In the second warehouse his art was on the ground floor. He created a loft for his bedroom space using ropes and pulleys to lift a bed, a one hundred gallon aquarium, a Lazy Boy chair and a TV to a second story. It reminded me of his man cave at age eight. After spending a night at his place on a mat on the floor in a narrow space between a drum set, piano and paint cans, I was concerned about his sleeping arrangement in the loft.

"Dave, I am worried about you painting all night and then climbing up that free standing two story ladder to reach your bed."

"Oh Mom, you worry too much, don't be paranoid, I'm fine."

Alas after several years, this warehouse too was going to be torn down. This time Dave's dad helped him buy a two thousand square foot home. It's made out of redwood sitting in the midst of a towering redwood forest near Santa Cruz, California.

Once when I was visiting I went to the San Jose museum and saw a sign that said they were looking for local artists to display their work. I saw some Jackson Pollock paintings on their walls and thought, "I think my son's are better than these."

I said, "Dave I think you might want to show your work there."

"Na, I'm not interested Mom."

That's the same thing he said to me when I told him an art gallery in Los Gatos, California asked me to have him come in when I told the manager my son painted abstracts like I saw in her window. I have a feeling someday, maybe after my son and I are gone, he'll be discovered and become famous.

He has recently followed in my photography footsteps. After a day of teaching in the San Jose school system, he and his canine buddy, Blew, an Australian Healer, head to the beach with a camera. I love his pink sunsets, one taken from inside a cave. My favorite is a reflection of pastel colors glistening on wet sand next to a towering wave broken into a thousand prisms as it hits a rock.

After seeing some of his photos I said, "Dave, I love the light and color you captured in your photos but I am concerned where you are standing to get those wave shots. I hope you aren't so close to the edge that you get washed out to sea."

"Ah Mom, if I get washed away, I'll have gone doing what I love."

I guess I can understand what he told me because I was thinking the same thing this week when I had the opportunity to do a photoshoot from a small experimental plane. As we were coming in for a landing, the speaker announced, "Fuel is low, fuel is low." I thought, "Well if I go this way, I will have died doing something I love, photographing nature, mountains and sea."

All the members of my family are interesting but maybe Dave's expression of art though the years is why I think he is the most interesting person in my family.

WRITE A STORY ABOUT YOUR GRANDMOTHER

by JIM WEATHERLY

MY GRANDMA IS SAND and dead seas and camels and cassette tapes. She traveled the Holy Lands recording all the sights and sounds and peoples she encountered along the footsteps of her lord and savior. She brought me back a wooden Bible, the envy of the snooty kids I was forced to attend Sunday school with back in the '80s, that I still own. I never paid attention to her inscription in the back of it when I was little. I just thought it was bad ass that she had written in a Bible—an act I thought was forbidden. It made her more of a rebel in my eyes.

A couple of my fellow Sunday school classmates, evil twins, always dominated the weekly Old and New Testament trivia contests that closed out mornings before heading back to our parents in the sanctuary. I was good at school, just not Sunday's version of it. I never answered the questions around the Bible's cast of characters correctly. Sloth. I was also bad at the speed races with our Bibles to find a specific chapter in the good book. The reward? Stickers. I wanted one. Lust. I wanted to fit in with the other kids, particularly the evil twins whose family was the toast of the temple. Envy.

Finally, I won one of those Sunday showdowns and got my sticker. I immediately sealed it to the back of my wooden Jerusalem-purchased Bible and strolled into the sanctuary, backside up, just to show off my trophy. Pride. I was going to keep winning and eventually cover that Bible in stickers. Greed. When my mother saw it, she freaked. At home after service, I remember her delicately trying to peel it off my Bible. (Her light fingernail scrapes into its soft wood are still visible when held in the right light.) I was mad at the time, but understand now. Wrath.

It was bigger than a silly sticker. And much cooler. Something I never should have been parading around any church. Gluttony. It belonged in a case, like a real trophy. Mom was right about the fact that someday I would want to stare at and hold it in my hands to remember Grandma. Today, in my home, that Bible sits on a bookshelf my grandpa built as a young man just beginning to tinker with tools. I treasure in having it and often read the inscription inside its back cover. My grandma is both where I get my knack for travel and love of learning. I know this now. And someday I am going to tattoo one of its handwritten sentences on my skin to forever remember my grandma, her sense of adventure, and my spirituality. Describing the journey to Bethlehem from Jerusalem in the night, she scrawled in green marker: "It was very cold and windy and quiet and beautiful." Life.

ABOUT THE WRITERS

GORDON ANDERSON's passion for writing dates back to "street poems" in the 1970s that turned into song lyrics. His current passion for haiku is bound in three volumes of *Gordito Haiku*. In addition, available on Amazon and at echnosprings pub.com are *Chosen Poems: Words of Love* (a collection of love poems) and *Looking Through the Knothole* (100 tritina poems).

GLEN BARBIERI is a US Navy veteran, an amateur scientist, and an avid science fiction fan. "I have no sense of humor. Just ask the three, invisible FBI agents who live under my bed," Glen says with a straight face.

CHERYLE HOSKINS BIGELOW is writing through the seventh draft of her life inspired by the fellowship of other Olympic Peninsula Authors. She is published monthly by the *Seniors Sunset Times* and covets time to work on her memoir about climbing the corporate ladder in high heels.

PATRICIA DEMARCO has spent a lifetime living, writing and working in close proximity to the natural world. Her blog, https://alpinelady.word press.com/, is a journey into the world of nature and wonder via prose, poetry, photographs, musings and magic.

BONNIE DICKMANN's writing career started as a Junior in high school when a teacher she loved and respected told her he enjoyed reading her essays. She has been published by the Wisconsin Department of Natural Resources as well as in *Stoneboat Literary Journal* and the *Creative Wisconsin Literary Journal*. She and her husband moved to Sequim in 2017. She hopes to publish a book soon.

SUSAN GEIS has always wanted to try writing, so when she and her husband retired to Sequim, a few years ago, she joined the Spontaneous Writing Sessions at the Sequim Library.

HEIDI HANSEN has been writing since college where she was editor of the weekly college newspaper. For the past ten years, she has honed her craft in writing and critique groups. She enjoys entertaining audiences at open mic events and has recently published two books of short stories—*A Slice of Life* and *A Second Slice*. She is currently working on a novel and a memoir.

DIANNE L. KNOX loves living with her rescue Lab-Rott mix, Kita, over-looking The Strait…while looking over her other loves—reading, hiking, Tai Chi, friends, and, oh, yes, writing.

JUDY LARIMORE is a photographer, artist and author. In December 2017 she became an author of a children's book about her horse, Jazz. Featured in the story are photographs taken on their rides over fifteen years from beaches to mountain tops. An upcoming series is entitled: THE ADVENTURES OF JUDY AND JAZZ. Her interest in writing began with winning a Kansas Club Author's contest in 1975.

PHILIP R. LIBOTT worked for the State of Washington as an employment counselor for 35 years, then retired and worked for another 4-plus years at Peninsula College as an Instructional Technician at the Sequim Education Center. He is stepping-up his creative writing activities, and increasing his participation in Clallam County literary and thespian activities.

ANNE LIZBORNE was a Rodeo Barrel Racer until age 18, when she developed a latent allergy to horses. That was the end of horses, but Charley's picture still hangs on her wall to this day, the one horse Anne will never forget. At age 24, Anne began solo traveling the world, always taking paint supplies and a travel journal to record her adventures. At age 70, Anne began writing the story of her life. The adventure goes on…

RUTH MARCUS loves to encourage writers to write. Her poetry has been published in the 2017 *WA129 Anthology*, *Cirque* (a literary journal for the North Pacific Rim), *Tidepools*, and *Last Wednesday: a Pacific Northwest Anthology of Poetry*. Her most recent book, *Haiku & Mandala: The Wedding of Ancient Art* showcases imagistic poetry and hand-drawn mandalas.

TRUDY MCFARLAND's first and foremost passion is for Jesus Christ and her family. She also loves to write and edit. To her surprise and pleasure, her poetry was published in two *Rainshadow Poetry Anthologies* sponsored by OTA. She is currently in an online school working towards her Associates Degree.

GEORGE MILLER, a Colorado native, retired as an engineer. He has dabbled in sales, construction, and research and development through his working life. Now he dabbles in his long-ignored passion for writing.

NEVI MILLER is semi-retired. She worked many years as an executive assistant in corporations and now substitutes for Sequim Schools. She dabbles in art and gardening.

TERRY MOORE's interests and employments have been varied and challenging, from farm to petroleum refinery, military base to missile silo, laboratory to cattle ranch, aircraft to sailboat. His writings are rich from many perspective—human and non-human, even from previous and future lifetimes. His published work includes a collection of poems and short stories titled *FICTION, mostly.*

VYKKI MORRISON started her life in the magical state of Vermont, then chose another magical state, Washington, to follow her dreams. She has been writing for almost five decades, and hopes to continue for another fifty years.

COLIN SELLWOOD was born in England, reared in New Zealand, then came to America as a young man. In his late thirties he was asked to write a pamphlet on how to coach soccer. Realizing that he liked to write, the pamphlet turned into a published book, *How to Have Fun and Play Better Soccer.* Since then, bringing up three children and running a business takes up most of his time.

LILY TODD started life in the Rocky Mountains of Montana. Her hobbies include reading, writing and observing people. Continuing her father's love of pranks, Lily likes to write stories with a surprise punch at the end.

JIM WEATHERLY is an aspiring good person, artist, activist; a cleaner-cut hippie, defender of the scrappy, husband, and—yes—even a professional (when necessary). Born Missourian, Jim is thankful to have found Sequim where seagulls sometimes hitchhike on cattle and there are no shortages of tall trees and open seas.

AFTERWORD

NOW THAT YOU have read samples of spontaneous writings, are you willing to experiment? Willing to write using the prompts in this book? Would it be useful to make a weekly or monthly commitment to this writing process?

Prompts are everywhere. Use magazine headlines, or open the dictionary and randomly point to three words. Incorporate them into your 10-minute writing. Select a photograph in a magazine or another image that catches your eye. Write a story based on the photo. Listen to people talk in a cafe or on a street corner. Use a line of their dialogue to create a story. Or, go to a park and let nature inspire spontaneous poetry.

Uncensored and unencumbered by your critical voice, relax and write. Experiment. Change the length of writing times— 5-minutes, 10-minutes, 20-minutes.

Who knows, your writings may become polished short-short stories, poems, and memoir chapters—even months or years later. That's part of spontaneous writing. Let it evolve. Relax and enjoy!

———